"I see you're getting an early start."

Ben turned to fall into step beside Caitlin. "May I join you? I'm trespassing. Do you mind?"

"Mind? Of course not! Why should I?" She looked up, puzzled.

"Your grandmother didn't, either. That's why I'm over here, I guess. I'm used to rambling pretty much wherever I want. Sometimes I feel like the whole end of this valley belongs to me," he went on, his words light, but Caitlin could sense the underlying edge. She frowned and looked down at the path. "I just wondered if the new owner might object."

"Heavens no. I like the company!" It was true. "Why? Don't you like people on your place?"

"No." His answer was cold and perfectly clear. Caitlin suddenly remembered seeing the No Hunting, No Trespassing signs posted all along the wooded property that bordered hers to the north.

"Why not?" She couldn't help it—she was curious. But neither did she miss Ben's swift glance and sudden frown. She could almost read his mind: *Nosy neighbor.*

"You might say I value my privacy."

Dear Reader:

Happy July! It's a month for warm summer evenings, barbecues and—of course—the Fourth of July. It's a time of enjoyment and family gatherings. It's a time for romance!

The fireworks are sparkling this month at Silhouette Romance. Our DIAMOND JUBILEE title is *Borrowed Baby* by Marie Ferrarella, a heartwarming story about a brooding loner who suddenly becomes a father when his sister leaves him with a little bundle of joy! Then, next month, don't miss *Virgin Territory* by Suzanne Carey. Dedicated bachelor Phil Catterini is determined to protect the virtue of Crista O'Malley—and she's just as determined to change her status as "the last virgin in Chicago." Looks like his bachelorhood will need the protection instead as these two lovers go hand in hand into virgin territory.

The DIAMOND JUBILEE—Silhouette Romance's tenth anniversary celebration—is our way of saying thanks to you, our readers. To symbolize the timelessness of love, as well as the modern gift of the tenth anniversary, we're presenting readers with a DIAMOND JUBILEE Silhouette Romance title each month, penned by one of your favorite Silhouette Romance authors. In the coming months, writers such as Annette Broadrick, Lucy Gordon, Dixie Browning and Phyllis Halldorson are writing DIAMOND JUBILEE titles especially for you.

And that's not all! There are six books a month from Silhouette Romance—stories by wonderful authors who time and time again bring home the magic of love. During our anniversary year, each book is special and written with romance in mind. July brings you *Venus de Molly* by Peggy Webb—a sequel to her heartwarming *Harvey's Missing.* The second book in Laurie Paige's poignant duo, *Homeward Bound,* is coming your way in July. Don't miss *Home Fires Burning Bright*—Carson and Tess's story. And much-loved Diana Palmer has some special treats in store in the month ahead. Don't miss Diana's fortieth Silhouette—*Connal.* He's a LONG, TALL TEXAN out to lasso your heart, and he'll be available in August....

I hope you'll enjoy this book and all of the stories to come. Come home to romance—Silhouette Romance—for always!

Sincerely,

Tara Hughes Gavin
Senior Editor

JUDITH BOWEN

That Man Next Door

Silhouette Romance

Published by Silhouette Books New York

America's Publisher of Contemporary Romance

To my pioneer grandmothers,
Bessie Julia and Elizabeth,
whose example taught me
what it meant to persevere.

SILHOUETTE BOOKS
300 E. 42nd St., New York, N.Y. 10017

ISBN: 0-373-08732-2

First Silhouette Books printing July 1990

Printed in the U.S.A.

JUDITH BOWEN

met her husband when they were editing competing newspapers in British Columbia, and they were married in Gibraltar. She has enjoyed raising sheep and children in Fraser Valley and still spins wool, knits, weaves and puts up dozens of jars of preserves and pickles every year. Her interests include reading, regional cookery, volunteer work, gardening and of course, writing romances.

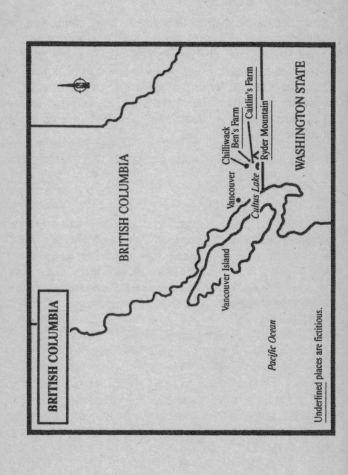

BRITISH COLUMBIA

BRITISH COLUMBIA

Vancouver Island

Pacific Ocean

Vancouver

Cultus Lake

Chilliwack
Ben's Farm
Caitlin's Farm
Ryder Mountain

WASHINGTON STATE

Underlined places are fictitious.

Chapter One

I thought I'd made it clear, Sam. You're to make her an offer she can't refuse.'' The man's cool gray eyes narrowed as he leaned back in his chair, turning to face the play of spring light and green in the poplars outside the study window. He frowned into the receiver, yanked impatiently at the tie knotted around his neck and listened, his lips thinned in irritation.

"Damn!" The chair thumped down. "What do you mean she won't sell? I want that farm, Sam, and I intend to get it." He laughed shortly. "Yeah, sure. She's not married? Maybe I will if it comes to that. Time I got around to it anyway. What kind of takeover would you call that?'' He laughed again and ran one hand through his dark hair, leaving it in disarray, then massaged the back of his neck briefly before flicking open a couple of shirt buttons, his red silk tie dangling carelessly down his shirtfront.

"Look." His voice hardened slightly. "Do what you have to do to get that property, Sam. That's what I pay you for."

He put the receiver down carefully and sat for a moment staring at it. Then, with a sigh, he got to his feet and walked toward the window, a tall, lean figure in superbly cut trousers and vest. His jacket had been thrown across a chair on the other side of the room. He leaned on the window frame.

There it was, stretching up behind him like a slumbering giant asleep for a million years, its profile hard against the sky. He loved this mountain. It was his refuge, his source of peace and tranquility, where he came to put his fast-lane life behind him. Ryder Mountain was private. It was where he belonged.

And there was only that one miserable stretch of stony soil that didn't belong to him between here and the summit. His neighbor was dead now and he was sorry for that; he'd loved the old lady like the grandmother he couldn't remember ever having. But now he had the chance to buy the farm she hadn't wanted to sell.

He turned away from the window, a frown marring his handsome features, a shadow in his eyes. Now some damned heir had come along, some granddaughter. And she didn't want to sell, either.

He grimaced, stretched and moved toward the door of the study, grabbing his jacket as he went. He wanted that farm. And one way or another, by damn, he was going to get it.

"Ouch!" The slim jeans-clad young woman dropped the rock she was lifting, and dark hair fell forward to cover her cheek as she bent to examine the damage inflicted on her middle finger. She studied roughened hands and broken fingernails ruefully and turned a little, her back to the dying sun.

"That's the second one nearly ripped to the quick," she said out loud in a conversational tone, apparently to herself. But an elderly Border collie that had been lying half-hidden in the shadows to one side of the broken ground, head down as sharp eyes followed the peregrinations of a small toad, looked up briefly, ears pricked, tail thumping once, then settled back down.

"And that's only on the one hand." She looked up, then, her blue eyes alight as she surveyed this—her very own farm, and immediately, her garden. She regarded the old dog with affection. True, you could hardly call it a garden yet. But it would be in time.

She bent to the wheelbarrow, half-full of fieldstones she'd picked out of the thin soil, her mind humming with visions of the stone fence she would build. She'd be able to see the fence from the parlor windows of the old farmhouse. And Caitlin Forrest liked to look out her windows and see things like stone fences and apple trees in blossom, and the big dark hulk of Ryder Mountain behind her to the south, and the sweet flanks of jersey cows grazing in clover. Her cows, her clover.

Thank goodness she hadn't sold out. Over her shoulder she called, "Lot you care, eh, Macleary?" The dog's tail thumped once more.

A few moments later Caitlin noticed that the old collie was sitting up on his haunches, ears pricked, attention turned to the hill. She glanced to the dark line of cedar and fir and white pine behind her.

"What's up there, old fella?" The tiniest flicker of apprehension ran through her as she searched the slope for whatever had taken the old dog's interest. After all, she was alone here, her nearest neighbors the van Holsts, a five-minute walk away. They had urged her to call on them for anything, anything at all that she might need at any time. But she could hardly rush over to tell them that Macleary thought he saw something up the hill. It was probably a squirrel or a rabbit or one of the dozens of mule deer that shared these upland pastures with the jerseys.

Ha! They'd really have her pegged for a city slicker then. Being on her own hadn't worried Caitlin when she'd decided to sublet her Vancouver apartment and move up to the little mountain farm her grandmother had left her, at the head of the Fraser Valley. The more than generous bid to buy the farm—an anonymous offer made through her grandmother's solicitors—hadn't tempted her at all. After all, Grandma Bevan had lived here for years after Gramps died, managing very well on her own.

Well, Caitlin thought, grimacing a little, perhaps not all that well. When she'd come up with the rental moving van and made her first thorough survey of the property she remembered so well from summers spent there as a child, she'd been aghast at the state of disrepair: fences down in unused pastures, haying machinery out of order and so ancient there were no parts available, a battered 1975 Ford stock truck that looked like the newest piece of equipment on the place, a dim cobwebbed dairy, its stone walls and floor patched with dampness. The list had seemed endless.

But gradually, with limited funds and boundless enthusiasm and energy, Caitlin had made inroads on the neglect. She'd worked hard on painting and papering the old homestead and now had abandoned that effort temporarily in favor of the garden. If she wanted to eat her own homegrown produce out of her pantry and freezer this winter, she had to start planting as soon as possible.

"What a crazy place for a garden!" she mused aloud, not for the first time, bending again to her task. The soil was full of stones, and sow thistles and burdock had sprung up everywhere. But it was near the house and in full sun, and Caitlin had decided to keep it there.

Suddenly Macleary jumped to his feet and began barking furiously.

"Macleary! Hush now." The dog ignored her. Then Caitlin saw his shaggy black tail wave frantically, and she let out her breath. Unconscious tension eased a little from her shoulders as two big Irish setters broke from the line of trees on the hillside, their happy tongues lolling. One, its coat burnished copper in the evening sun, trotted over to inspect Caitlin. She patted a broad head, accepted a wet welcome on the back of her hand and put her hands on her hips to study the newcomers.

"And where did you pretty fellows come from? Friends of yours, are they, Macleary?"

"They're mine." The quiet words startled Caitlin and she swung around. She'd been so absorbed in the dogs that she hadn't seen the man follow them down the hill, but now she looked up, startled blue eyes meeting a steely gray gaze, curiously detached. Her rapid glance took in an impression of thick dark brown hair, slightly above average height and lean athletic build hinting at reserves of power, yet perfectly contained. If asked, Caitlin would not have been able to analyze her quick chaotic feeling.

"You live around here?" Caitlin wiped her hands on her jeans, then held one out in greeting. "I'm Caitlin Forrest."

The stranger hesitated for just the briefest of instants. Or had he? Perhaps she'd imagined it. Then he pulled one hand from the pocket of his dark green jacket and took hers. His handshake was firm and dry and brief. Yet she thought her hand retained the warmth of his long after he'd jammed it back into his pocket. Confused by the odd sensation, Caitlin repeated her query.

"Live around here?"

"Just over there." The man shrugged one shoulder and indicated the north with a nod of his head. "I guess we're neighbors, Miss Forrest. Hey, there, down, Hobo.'' He bent to ruffle the ears of the dog that had bounded over and jumped on him.

''They're lovely dogs.'' Caitlin was at an uncharacteristic loss for words. The man had seemed polite enough, although just barely. And he seemed oddly formal. So much for rural bonhomie! When he straightened—the setter sitting now and gazing up adoringly—a half smile played about his firm, well-shaped lips. Caitlin could see the smile was reserved for the dog. Humph!

''Well—?'' As she spoke, his cool glance flicked to her, then to the dog again. ''Uh—if you'll excuse me, I want to get in a few more loads while it's still light.'' She bent down for another rock and threw it onto the wheelbarrow. A few yards away the man stood and watched her, frowning slightly.

Caitlin heaved at the handles of the wheelbarrow and marched off, her path back to the dairy already well marked in the sod. She reached the halfway point of her planned fence marked with a series of sticks, put the barrow down and started heaving rocks off.

The nerve! she thought, wiping the beads of perspiration on her upper lip with a plaid flannel sleeve. I mean, naturally I'm for women's lib and all that, and of course women can do any kind of work they darn well want to, but what kind of man would stand there with his hands in his pockets, watching a woman haul rocks? The least he could do is take his—his high-class bird dogs and go home. Anyone who knew her well would have recognized the dangerous glint in her eye as she made her way back again. But the man seemed oblivious.

''Would you like a hand with that?''

His unexpected offer was quiet and serious, in the same neutral tones he'd used in making himself known to her, and instantly her anger evaporated. His eyes met hers and held, and for a split second Caitlin caught her breath as she felt something spring to life between them. Something that had nothing to do with the hills or the forest or the dying sun or the immediate work of hauling stones. Then she tore her gaze away, strangely disquieted.

"I'd love some help—neighbor." She stressed the last word, but her impish grin took the sting out of her emphasis.

"Ben," he said, holding out his hand again, this time a smile crinkling the tanned skin beside his eyes, warming their cool gray depths, softening his features.

"Caitlin." Caitlin took his hand once more and again felt his heat go through her.

"Right. I'll help you load, then I'll push the barrow over. That where you want it?" He pointed to where she'd dropped her last load and she nodded.

They worked in silence for a while. Ben had taken off his jacket and rolled up the sleeves of his cotton shirt. The muscles of his forearms and shoulders shifted smoothly and rhythmically under the thin fabric as he pushed the heavy load over to the dairy, and Caitlin found herself suddenly shy as she walked beside him.

Who was this man? He wasn't a farmer, judging by the expensive cut of his boots and jacket, and his hands, though hard, were not the hands of a man who milked cows or wrestled bales of hay around. She'd probably never find out, she thought, if she relied on him to volunteer information. He hadn't even told her his last name!

"Why are you moving the stones over here?" He stood up straight after dumping the load and looked around at the ramshackle house, the stone dairy, then down at her.

"I'm building a stone fence."

"A stone fence!"

"Yes."

"What's wrong with barbed wire? Rails?"

"What's wrong with stone?" She returned, stung at the implied incredulity in his voice. He looked at her sharply, then away, his narrowed gaze moving to the old homestead with its sagging porch, the front amass with old-fashioned hollyhocks in bud.

"Nothing, I guess. Cheap enough, but a lot of hot work." His gaze traveled slowly, deliberately, down her slim frame, taking in her long dark hair in wild disarray, most of it escaped from the pins she'd used to fasten it back, her faded jeans, her new tan lace-up work boots, freshly scuffed. He jerked his head down, suppressing a quick smile.

"Steel toes, I hope."

"Of course." Caitlin picked up the wheelbarrow and trundled it back.

"I was watching you, you know. On the hill." She glanced sharply up at him as he walked beside her, catching his look of inner amusement. "I was trying to figure out what you were up to."

"And couldn't you?"

"No." He hesitated, then gave her a sudden grin that made Caitlin catch her breath again. "That's why I thought I'd come down and ask." Was he telling her that if he hadn't been a little curious he would have stayed up there in the woods, watching her, and not made himself known? What an odd thing to do!

"Well, it seems perfectly straightforward to me," she said, dropping the wheelbarrow's handles. They were back in the garden, standing very close to each other, and Caitlin involuntarily stepped back a pace. "I'm taking stones out so that I can plant a garden here."

"Hmm. 'And why isn't she just taking them to one side, near the garden, in a pile?' I asked myself," Ben went on, more to himself, it seemed, than her. "But now I find she wants to build a stone fence." He started loading more stones in silence, a slight smile on his face. "Sounds pretty permanent."

"My grandmother told me that it was silly to move things like stones more than once. When you're doing it by hand. You know, it wastes too much energy or something," Caitlin said, disregarding his last remark. Inexplicably, she wanted him to understand what she was doing with the stones. It had something to do with why she was here at Hollyhock Farm, not back in Vancouver at her job in the medical lab, and it suddenly was important that he know that.

"Ah..." Ben lifted the load easily and they started back again. "Sounds like a practical idea for a homesteader." Caitlin lengthened her stride to keep up to his longer one.

"Well—" She felt her feathers ruffle a little. Is that what he thought she was? Part of the back-to-the-land crowd? "Anyway, she said when you've got stones to move, you should first of all decide what you're going to do with them and only move them once. So I decided to build a fence."

"I see," Ben said, and glanced down at her, at the smile that lit up mobile features and brought warm sparks to blue eyes. He studied her gravely for a few seconds, his eyes taking in the freckles, the clear brow, the high cheekbones and the thick dark lashes that dropped now to shadow her cheek. His eyes darkened to slate as a delicate pink flush rose from her nape, then he frowned and looked away.

Caitlin cursed her sophomoric response to his curiously detached survey and bent to the task. She never blushed! Thank goodness they were nearly done.

They dumped the last load and Caitlin politely asked him if he'd like a cup of tea, but the reserved air he'd arrived with returned and he declined as politely. With a call to his dogs and a brief wave, he turned and faded into the dusk as silently as he'd arrived.

Caitlin climbed the steps slowly. A hot shower would be marvelous, she thought, but the conveniences of the homestead only ran to a big old claw-footed cast-iron bathtub connected to a very small and temperamental hot-water tank.

"I wonder what a new hot-water tank costs?" she mused aloud to Macleary, who had stretched out beside the big kitchen range and was regarding her with intelligent eyes. The features of her new neighbor, his cool gray eyes, his aloof manner floated absently into her mind, then firmly she thought of her dwindling bank account. Hot-water tanks! Heavens, she'd never given hot-water tanks a thought before. She sighed. A new hot-water tank would mean a big bill from the plumber.

That was the thing, Caitlin thought, a few days later as she sat over her breakfast: money.

She had already been out at the barn at five o'clock to help Lucas van Holst, her neighbor and savior, literally. What had she known about milking cows? Not much three weeks ago, but quite a lot now, she thought with some pride.

Caitlin's dream was to have Hollyhock Farm become a small cottage dairy that would turn out gourmet cheeses for the Vancouver restaurant and delicatessen trade. Lucas thought she was crazy.

"Ya mean you're goin' to milk these here cows every day, mornin' and night, day in and day out?" He pushed back the visor cap he wore, with Fraser Feeds printed in orange letters across the front, and scratched his grizzled head. Settling the cap more firmly than before, he went on. "Cows don't take no holidays, young lady, and you won't neither if you take 'em on. Criminy!"

And he'd hitched his thumbs in his overalls and leaned back on his heels, looking down at her, all five-and-a-half feet of her. He shook his head. "Let the co-op take yer milk or ring up the Glendinning boys." They were the local stockbrokers.

"But I won't have more than twenty cows, Lucas. At the most," she'd said, protesting at his skepticism. Caitlin sighed. No one took her plans seriously. Her parents had smiled indulgently, regarding this as just the latest in a long line of their youngest daughter's harebrained schemes, but had given her their blessing, certain she'd come around within six months.

She couldn't really blame them: she'd tried everything else, from keeping bees on the rooftop of her apartment building to going partners with a friend on a mail-order dried herb business. Her sister, Sharon, had tried to talk her into accepting the unexpected offer on the farm and investing the proceeds, pointing out the advantages of staying at her job, her pension benefits, her seniority at the lab. Sharon had even suggested there might be a junior position in her husband's accounting firm if she wanted a career switch.

No, all Caitlin wanted was lots of fresh air, Hollyhock Farm and a chance to make it on her own. Deep down she sometimes wondered if that's why Grandma Bevan had left her the farm. She and the old lady had been special friends, kindred spirits. Her grandmother would have known she wouldn't sell out to the first bidder.

No, there was a niche market in Vancouver for high-quality gourmet dairy items, and now that she'd inherited the farm, the jerseys and Macleary, she planned to fill it. This time, Caitlin vowed, it was going to be different.

But the farm was a long way from metamorphosing into a modern small dairy, the kind she'd need if she wanted to realize her dream. For that metamorphosis she needed money and plenty of it.

Caitlin piled her breakfast dishes in the sink and stepped out onto the old wooden veranda, letting the screen door slam behind her. She whistled for Macleary, and in a few seconds the black-and-white collie bounded around the corner of the barn toward her.

"Coming, old boy? Let's go over to Flat Pond to see if I can fix that fence." She slung her rucksack onto her back.

"Good morning!"

Caitlin shaded her eyes against the brightness. It was the neighbor she'd met in her garden last week, following Macleary around the side of the barn. He stopped in front of her, and she looked up, meeting gray eyes warm with amusement.

She hoped her quick blush of pleasure had been attributed to surprise, if he'd noticed it at all. And, of course, that's all it had been. Besides Lucas and the agriculture rep she'd been dealing with, Caitlin hadn't seen anyone in the past week.

"I see you're getting an early start. May I join you?" He turned to fall into step beside her, stooping once to pat the leaping, frolicking Macleary. Then he plucked a long stalk of timothy and chewed the end of it thoughtfully. "I'm trespassing. Do you mind?"

"Mind? Of course not! Why should I?" She looked up, puzzled.

"Your grandmother didn't, either. That's why I'm over here, I guess. I'm used to rambling pretty much wherever I want. Sometimes I feel like the whole end of this valley belongs to me," he went on, his words light but with an underlying edge. Caitlin frowned and looked down at the path. "I just wondered if the new owner might object."

"Heaven's, no. I like the company!" She laughed. It was true. The morning, already perfect, had taken on a fresher, brighter dimension all of a sudden. "Why? Don't you like people on your place?"

"No." His answer was cold and perfectly clear.

Caitlin suddenly remembered seeing the No Hunting, No Trespassing signs posted all along the wooded property that bordered hers to the north, and all along the road frontage a mile or so before reaching Hollyhock Farm.

"Why not?" She couldn't help it—she was curious. But neither did she miss Ben's swift glance and sudden frown. Nosy neighbor, she could almost read his mind.

"You might say I value my privacy." Ben's voice held a curious flatness, a faint warning that he didn't care to be questioned further on the topic.

Halfway across the field, knee-deep in daisies and buttercups, Caitlin turned to look back at Hollyhock Farm. In the silence broken only by the whir of a dragonfly, wings ashimmer in the clear morning sun, and the rasp of grasshoppers as they ground out their summer songs in the deep grass, the little farm looked asleep at the foot of Ryder Mountain. She took a few steps backward, a satisfied smile on her face. The hard work she'd put in showed in the fresh whitewash of the paddock fences, the tidiness of the shrubbery around the homestead, the— "Oh!" Hard hands gripped her shoulders as Ben caught her from behind and held her for a moment. She heard his deep laugh. For an instant Caitlin was very aware of the length of his body against hers and shivered.

"Hold it!" He released her, and she turned to where he had bent to one side of the path. "Look here." A blue flower with delicately fringed petals dotted a patch of moist ground. Ben touched the flower gently with one finger.

"*Gentiana crinita*. Fringed gentian. This one's blooming a bit early. You nearly stepped on it."

"Are you a botanist?" She squatted beside him to study the little flower, very conscious of his strong thigh, taut in khaki drill pants, brushing hers lightly.

"No. It's a hobby of mine, though." He paused, a slight frown on his face. "This is an endangered species, Caitlin. You're lucky to find a few here. Overzealous collectors have pretty well wiped it out, I'm afraid."

Caitlin stood and stepped back onto the path. He straightened, too, and lifted one hand in an easy gesture to tuck back a lock of her hair that had fallen forward. "Very like the color of your eyes," he said quietly, smiling.

Startled, she met his eyes, then quickly looked away. She decided to pretend she hadn't heard that remark. "So you're not a scientist?"

They continued toward the pond. "No."

"A farmer?"

"No."

"A writer? An artist?" She recalled the strength, the well-manicured squareness of his long, lean fingers.

"No."

She glanced up. He was smiling after all, not offended by her attempt to prize information from him.

"A hermit?"

"I wouldn't like to think so."

"You're some kind of outlaw!"

"No." He was grinning now, his gray eyes alive with amusement as they caught and held hers.

She looked at the path again quickly, unable to stop the sudden rush of her pulse. This neighbor—whoever he was— was having a maddening effect on her equanimity, she thought with dismay. She abandoned the guessing game.

They were approaching Flat Pond now, a low swampy area that had water in it during the rainy spring and winter and often dried to a sticky mix of marsh mud and grasses in the middle of summer. She swung her rucksack down.

"Mending fences?"

Caitlin looked up at him, squinting in the sun. "Yes. Grandma didn't keep up the place very well, much beyond the home pasture and the vegetable garden."

"If you're planning to fix up this place on your own, you've got your work cut out. Why don't you hire someone?"

"A man, I suppose you mean?" Caitlin snapped. Why did everyone think everything in life was divided into men's and women's work? It was true, people like her parents had always accepted the maxim. Her father would no more vacuum or prepare a meal for the family than fly to the moon, and her mother thought it was her duty to wait on her father hand and foot, always had. Someday, Caitlin hoped, she'd meet a man who could cook a meal as well as fix a fence, and then, just maybe, she'd—Caitlin suddenly flushed. Whatever was she thinking about!

"No. I didn't." His voice was cool. "I just meant you're going to need help to get this place fixed up, and I simply suggested one way to do it."

Caitlin was ashamed of the way she'd attacked him.

Ben walked over to a fence post and gave it a good push. The weathered cedar post tilted crazily. He tried the next one. It too wobbled, but the next one was firm. He walked back and stared down at her, a slight frown on his face.

"Got an axe? A hatchet?" He narrowed his eyes at her negative shake. "Just how were you planning to cut poles to shore up these posts? Half of them are rotten."

He sounded disgusted. Caitlin stood stiffly, her eyes a flash of blue as they met his. But what was the point in defiance? It's the truth, she thought, suddenly miserable. She didn't know a damn thing about fixing fences.

"I—I didn't know I'd need one," she said, swallowing hard. "I just thought I might have to tighten a few wires or—or put in some nails or something."

That was one of the problems she'd discovered since arriving at Hollyhock Farm: every task she set herself took three times as long as it should have, because she was learning everything by trial and error. What she wanted to do—start producing cheese the way she'd learned in a special course she'd taken last winter—was being delayed because there were so many other jobs that needed her immediate attention. Like fences that wouldn't hold cattle.

"Caitlin?" Ben took a step toward her, his expression blurring as she tried to clear sudden tears. Caitlin felt the heat of his hands through her muslin shirt as he grabbed her shoulders. She tried to step back, but his grasp was firm. She turned her head and blinked hard, reluctant to let him see her tears.

"Please! Let me alone." But her voice cracked and Ben took her chin roughly in one hard hand and turned her face toward him. Then, instantly tender, he wiped the few tears that had spilled over onto her cheeks with the side of his thumb.

"Caitlin—look at me."

She turned up brimming eyes to meet his, their usual cool detachment hot now with a fierce immediacy.

"Just what are you trying to prove up here, Caitlin Forrest? What kind of game are you playing at?"

He shook her slightly, but she just stared at him, puzzled at his vehemence, her whole being shockingly aware of his warmth, his nearness, the feel of his hands on her shoulders.

He swore softly under his breath. "Why do you want to build a stone fence, for God's sake? What are you doing up here? Why aren't you in Vancouver holding down a nice job, where you clearly belong? Why!"

Why was she here? Blinking rapidly, Caitlin told him in a few halting sentences about her dreams for her cottage dairy, how she wanted to escape from Vancouver, how the city had been choking the joy out of her life for years now, how Grandma Bevan leaving her this farm had been a dream come true.

As she talked, Caitlin studied Ben's face, and not once did she detect derision or disbelief or even amusement.

He was watching her closely, his gray eyes calm again, taking in her shy happiness, her innocent belief in an enterprise that he knew went against all odds. He watched the mobile, sensuous mouth as she talked, the play of emotions across her fine features.

Then she stopped and looked up at him expectantly. Had he understood? He was very still, his eyes darker than she'd ever seen them.

"Caitlin." His voice was quiet.

"Yes?"

"Do you want me to help you?"

"Help me?" She looked up quickly, to meet his gaze again, alight this time with amusement and something softer and deeper.

"Help fix the fence, of course."

She looked at the sagging fence. The top wire was down and the posts Ben had tested still leaned drunkenly. She needed any help she could get. Trying to do everything herself, depending on no one, was just foolish pride. She'd need to swallow that pride to ask the bank for a loan, and she'd need to swallow that pride now.

"Yes, Ben," she said quietly, her eyes once again turning to his. "I'd like that."

"Right. Where're the keys to your truck?" Ben's voice had taken on a new firmness and authority. She told him and watched him stride away.

Hours later, Caitlin tossed the leather gloves she'd been wearing into the back of Ben's pickup—he hadn't trusted her old Ford to make it across the field—and leaned stiffly against the tailgate, watching as Ben drove in the last staple with a few expert hammer blows. He tugged at the wire to test its tautness, then turned to her with a wide grin.

"That should do it." He picked up his discarded shirt from the front seat of the truck and wiped the sweat from his face and bare chest. "Tired?"

Watching him, Caitlin again felt something unknown and a little frightening stir deep within her, as she had several times that afternoon working alongside Ben, handing him tools, driving in staples, helping to set crosspieces and tighten wires. She deliberately averted her eyes from his gleaming torso as he casually donned the shirt, leaving the front hanging open.

"Ooh," she groaned, straightening. "Every muscle I own aches and some I didn't even know I had!" She bent to help gather up the tools and stow them in the truck box.

Ben laughed. "A meal and a hot shower and you'll be good as new." His eyes lowered to take in her soiled denims, her thin shirt clinging to her breasts and back with perspiration, and Caitlin felt her cheeks burn.

"That's a nasty one," he said, moving beside her and lifting her hand to examine a deep scratch on her forearm she'd got from the barbed wire. "We'll put something on that when we get home."

"It's all right. Really," Caitlin said, pulling away. She found his touch and the heady male scent of him so near her unsettling. To her surprise, he didn't let her go. He pulled her in closer and put his other arm around her in a tight, hard embrace. She looked up, her heart racing. He was grinning down at her, a relaxed, happy look on his face.

"You're a good worker, partner."

Was he going to kiss her? She averted her eyes suddenly, aware of the color that had flooded into her cheeks, and caught sight of his watch in his shirt pocket.

"The cows!" Caitlin wailed. "Oh, Ben. What kind of a farmer am I? I forgot all about the cows!" She reached for his watch and stepped back. "Quarter past six!" She forgot her weariness in her anxiety to get back to the jerseys. She knew they'd be lined up at the barn, waiting to get in, lowing, udders swollen with milk.

"Relax." Ben grinned and opened the passenger door of the pickup for her, then went around to the driver's side, tossing his gloves onto the seat between them.

"Relax! How can I relax! I'm supposed to be a farmer now, I've got cows to look after. I've got to get back—right away." She watched Ben, half-twisted toward her, arm across the seat back, as he looked out the rear window of the pickup, negotiating reverse until he could turn the truck around in the field. She watched the play of muscles in his forearms as he shifted into first, then second. Reluctantly her eyes lingered over the smooth planes of his chest, lightly covered with dark silky hair, the broad flat curve of ribs that she could see under the open shirt. Ben didn't reply until the truck had picked up a little speed, then he turned to her, eyes gleaming. She flushed, knowing he'd been aware of her appraisal.

"Hot in here?" His voice held a low note of amusement.

"Yes." Annoyed, Caitlin turned her flushed face to the window, rolled it down and leaned out for a moment, letting the coolness fan her cheeks.

"You can forget about the cows. They've been taken care of."

"What!" Caitlin jerked her head back into the truck. Ben was studying the ground ahead as they bumped over grassy hummocks on their way back to the roadway.

"Lucas milked them."

"How—how do you know? I didn't ask him to milk them tonight. He's counting on me to show up."

"I asked him."

"You did!"

"When I went back for the truck, I phoned and asked him to take over for you this evening," Ben said. "I knew it would take all afternoon to fix that fence, maybe longer." He turned calmly to her, one eyebrow raised as though wondering what in the world she was getting so steamed up about.

Chapter Two

Caitlin saw red. First he had taken charge of her fence-mending—well, she reminded herself, she'd needed his experience there—then he'd started giving orders about her cows!

"Just what's going on here? Those are my cows and I'm in charge. What makes you think you can arrange for Lucas to take over?" She glared at him. "It's one thing to bring over your own fence posts and pickup and all your tools—although of course I intend to pay you for them—but it's quite another to—"

"Caitlin!" Ben thundered, startling her into silence. He pulled the truck over to the shoulder of the road and hit the brakes hard. Then, coolly, deliberately, he turned off the engine and looked at her, his gray eyes icy cold. "Let's settle this now, shall we?"

It was as though the easy camaraderie of the afternoon had never been. A pang of regret swept through Caitlin, then she grabbed for the door handle. But Ben was faster and his hand closed hard over hers, stopping her.

"Listen to me," he ordered. His half-bare chest was pressed hard against her shoulder, the tanned satiny skin just inches from her mouth.

She could feel his warm breath on her damp forehead. She felt grimy and sweaty and hot. Reluctantly she looked up and faced him, her breath shallow, her eyes furious.

"Now," he continued, his face close to hers. "Let's be reasonable."

Caitlin swallowed. If only he would move back, let go of her hand—she couldn't think straight with his weight half across her, pinning her to the truck seat like this. She stopped struggling and closed her eyes for a moment, reining in her anger and willing herself to relax.

Immediately Ben let go of her and sat back, glancing once at the road, then in the rearview mirror, then at her. "Okay?"

She nodded.

"Now. Here's the way I saw it: You wanted me to help fix your fence and I knew from experience—" here he shot her a faintly derisive look "—that it was a good half-day job for both of us. Right?" He lifted one eyebrow, waited, and she nodded. "So I called Lucas to take over because I knew it was important to you to get the job done." He paused, then went on, driving the point home. "Am I right?"

Caitlin nodded again. Of course he was right. He'd only been trying to help her. It wasn't such a big deal after all, just that her temper and prickly pride had made her bristle at the way he'd taken charge. Everything he said made perfect sense. There was no way she could have contacted Lucas herself anyway, she had been out at Flat Pond.

Be reasonable, he had said. She sighed, and some of the tension left her shoulders. Ben started up the truck again and swung onto the road. For a few moments Caitlin stared out the window, roadside tansy and fireweed in full bloom going by in a blur of yellow and purple. She blinked. Ben was right. Why had she jumped on him like that?

"Ben?"

Her voice was small. Ben looked over at her sharply, half-frowning, took in her weariness, her tousled head resting against the back of the seat as she looked at him, her small scratched-up hands resting on her thighs. He was conscious of a reluctant growing admiration for the young woman beside him, for her courage and stamina and determination in the face of every challenge. Even him.

"Yes?"

"I'm sorry. For snapping at you like that. I—I shouldn't have."

Their eyes met, held, and suddenly the afternoon held joy again for Caitlin, and for the man beside her, although neither quite understood why.

Ben smiled suddenly, his teeth a flash of white in his tanned face. "Hmm. Forget it."

Forgiven, smiling, Caitlin turned again to the window. "Hey! You missed my turnoff." They were well past the lane to Hollyhock Farm, in fact were approaching the wooded lane that marked the entrance to Ben's property. Ben just grinned and slowed to make the turn.

"Have you forgotten your truck?"

"Oh, yeah." Caitlin's heart had given an odd little skip when she'd realized that he was taking her to his place, and now it steadied. Of course—her old Ford. He'd left it at his place when he'd gone for his pickup.

They made their way slowly along a shaded curving track, the graveled surface dappled with the shadows of huge alders and maples and the occasional cedar and Sitka spruce. On either side, the sparse mountain grasses and flowers grew like a carpet under the old trees. There was very little undergrowth. Caitlin was suddenly curious to see where her mysterious neighbor lived.

Half a mile on, they emerged into a clearing and Caitlin could see a small stretch of lawn where the driveway curved. Macleary barked from his position in the back of the pickup and was answered with a deep chorus as the two Irish setters bounded out. There was her old truck parked beside a silvery weathered outbuilding, perhaps a garage or small barn.

So this was where Ben lived. She took a deep breath. He had stopped the truck and sat back, studying her reaction with narrowed eyes. It was very quiet, just the whisper of the wind in the tall trees and the sharp ping of the truck's engine as it cooled.

"It's lovely!" Caitlin breathed. "What a beautiful place to live." She looked at the long, low lodge before her, built of logs, with a cedar shake roof and several massive fieldstone fireplaces, judging from the chimneys she could see. A veranda completely covered the western facade, set about with comfortable-looking upholstered wooden deck chairs and settees. Recovering from her initial surprise—she hadn't known what to expect—Caitlin turned to the man beside her. The lodge and its woodland setting suited him perfectly. It clearly was not a farmhouse.

"Care to have a look around?"

Ben's voice held a slightly different note, a guardedness, and she looked at him quickly. Lonely? Surely not. He was a man who had chosen this isolated place deliberately, for his own reasons, whatever they were. But Caitlin felt he particularly wanted to show her his house. Perhaps he was an architect and had designed it?

"Oh, Ben. Look at me!" She gestured down to her filthy jeans and boots. "I'm not in any shape to—"

"Come on then. What did I say about a good meal and a hot shower?" The prospect of a hot shower was very tempting. He was holding the door of the truck open for her.

"But I've got nothing to change into, I've—ouch!" She gingerly clung to the door of the truck as she eased herself out. Her muscles had all tightened into a sitting position. Ben stepped forward and with one smooth movement swung her up into his arms.

"It's settled then?" He grinned down at her, his face very close, his arms around her strong and secure and strangely comforting. Eyes wide, she nodded, for once too surprised to answer.

Half an hour later, Caitlin felt like a new woman. The spray had soothed her tired body until finally, feeling a bit guilty about using so much hot water, she had stepped out to dry herself with a huge fluffy towel. But when she'd looked around for her clothes, she discovered only a white cotton Japanese-style kimono where they had been. She slipped into the voluminous folds of the kimono and followed her nose to the kitchen.

"Mmm. Something smells delicious!" The enticing aroma of garlic and basil and fresh onions filled the sunny room where Ben, hair still damp from his shower, was standing at the countertop range, stirring something in a copper skillet. He was wearing a white T-shirt and clean faded denims, and an apron was tied around his waist. It was a masculine-looking striped affair, but it was definitely an apron.

Ben looked up and gave her an easy smile of welcome, and Caitlin felt a quick flutter in her midriff. How could she have ever thought those eyes cold? His gaze casually took her in from turbanned head to slim bare feet.

"Feel better?"

"Wonderful. I'd forgotten how marvelous a shower could be. I've just got an old tub at Hollyhock, and not a very big hot-water tank." Caitlin perched on a stool at the counter and watched his preparations. He was chopping fresh tomatoes and green pepper and had strips of ham in a small bowl to one side. His hands, lean and tanned, moved surely and swiftly with the big chef's knife.

"You look wonderful, Caitlin," he said quietly, and Caitlin's eyes flew to meet his. He studied her openly, taking in her flushed cheeks, the dark blue of her eyes and the darkness of her hair contrasting vividly with the white robe and towel on her head.

She felt a blush rising, adding to her color. Caitlin paid little attention to her looks, feeling inside that she'd never really changed from a gawky tomboy with skinned knees and a sunburned nose. She'd been the second daughter, so used to being outshone by her delicate blond elder sister, that compliments from men always surprised her and embarrassed her a little. She feigned a sudden interest in the pan.

"What are you making?"

"Pipérade. Like it?"

"Lovely." His unabashed competence in the kitchen surprised her. But then, men these days weren't at all like the previous generation, like her father, whose cooking talents had run the gamut from instant chicken soup to a fried egg—and that was it. Still, she mused, pipérade....

Ben dumped the tomatoes and peppers into the pan and gave everything a quick stir. Then he stepped back to reach for a first aid kit from a shelf above the wall oven.

"Here. Let me look at that." He pulled over a stool and sat astride it, facing her, their knees nearly touching. He took her hand gently and examined the scratch on her arm.

"Deep, but it looks clean. I'll just put some of this stuff on to make sure."

"Ouch!" Caitlin winced as Ben dabbed at the scratch with some reddish disinfectant. "Sorry. I'm an awful coward when it comes to this sort of thing."

"Hmm. I wouldn't have thought so." Ben regarded her solemnly, a slight smile tugging at the corners of his lips. "You don't strike me as being afraid of anything, Caitlin." Then he blew lightly on her wrist to dry the solution and dipped his head to place a quick warm kiss next to her injury. "All better now."

Caitlin had to suppress the sudden urge to put her hand on his head, to touch the damp dark hair, to feel its softness and crispness, to bury her fingers in it, to shape the warmth and the curve in her two hands....

"Ah, yes. Promises." Caitlin managed a smile at the childhood memory of the kiss that made everything better, desperately trying to quell the surge of feeling that had suddenly, inexplicably, overtaken her. Ben studied her for a long moment.

"Does it embarrass you? When I tell you how wonderful you look?"

Caitlin raised shocked eyes to his. This was not playing by the social rule book! He looked completely unperturbed, just faintly curious.

"What embarrasses me is you asking me if it embarrasses me! That's what embarrasses me," she returned roundly, feeling thoroughly flustered. His eyes had not left her face and now she saw his gaze travel deliberately down over her body, covered by the folds of the kimono. His kimono.

"You shouldn't. You're very beautiful." He stood and returned the first aid kit to the cupboard. "Surely, this isn't the first time a man's told you that."

"As a matter of fact, it isn't," she snapped, blue eyes flashing. "And where are my clothes, by the way?" Men!

"In the washing machine. But there's no rush." He grinned, as though he'd read her mind. "I have no immediate plans to unwrap you and make love to you—not when the pipérade is almost ready." He got up to stir the mixture again, smiling with inner amusement. "The laundry's first door on the left."

Caitlin followed his directions and transferred her clothes to the dryer, giving the door a satisfying slam. Men, all right! Except that she couldn't figure this one out. He seemed to know just what buttons to push with her, but he didn't follow up. So far, except for carrying her in from the truck—and he'd been scrupulously polite about setting her down at the bathroom door—and the quick hug in the field, he hadn't touched her. Yet he made her blood sing with his voice and his words and just the way he looked at her sometimes. Caitlin frowned and returned to the kitchen.

"Voilà!" He sprinkled the egg-and-vegetable mixture with ham strips and parsley and gave her a friendly smile, as though the interchange ham strips and parsley and gave her a friendly smile, as though the interchange of a few moments ago hadn't taken place. She followed him to a small kitchen nook overlooking the woodland. The table was already set with two places, and a bottle of wine was standing in the middle, uncorked.

"Mademoiselle." With a mock flourish, Ben whipped off his apron and held out her chair for her. Then he untucked her towel. Dark curls tumbled over her shoulders in damp disarray. "Hush, Caitlin," he said, smiling down at her opened mouth. "I like your hair like this. Besides, you want it to dry." He combed his fingers through her hair lightly, then took his place at the other side of the table.

What he'd said was only reasonable. Why did it feel, then, like something else altogether, completely unreasonable—his slight touch like a new yet familiar note in a slow and intricate overture, the mysterious secret resonances of courtship and love? Caitlin shook her head. Her imagination had run away with her completely!

"Wine?" He poured for them both, not waiting for an answer, then raised his glass. *"Bon appétit."*

The pipérade was delicious. She was famished and ate seconds with appreciation. She allowed him to pour her another glass of Chablis, then leaned back, replete, feeling extremely tired, extremely comfortable and extremely happy.

"More?"

"No, thank you. That was absolutely delicious, Ben." She lifted her wineglass and looked at him over the top. It occurred to her that she didn't know a thing about the man sitting across from her. "I'll admit, I'm very impressed."

"Impressed?"

Caitlin watched Ben lean back and look at her, frowning slightly, the delicate stemmed crystal cradled by his lean, strong hands. The hands that had spent the afternoon wielding a hammer and tugging at wire. Hands that—Caitlin shivered. She'd just had a vision of those hands, strong and sensitive, moving across a woman's skin— "With what?"

"With—with your domestic talents, of course. You're an excellent cook for one thing. And you do laundry."

He laughed. "Of course." It was said quietly, as though she should have expected as much. "One must take care of oneself, after all."

He looked out the window, eyes narrowed, and Caitlin suddenly had the feeling—again—that he was miles away from her. She leaned back and observed him quietly, the fingers of one hand absently smoothing crumbs on the table, the other still turning the wineglass gently. His strong profile was shadowed by his slight frown, the firm, sensuous mouth deliberately set, the jaw tight. Suddenly, as though he'd made some kind of decision, he drained his glass and turned to her.

"How about a quick tour? Or would you like to wander about by yourself while I put these in the dishwasher and make coffee? Or would you prefer to get dressed now and go home?" He raised one eyebrow. Caitlin laughed, a light happy sound that brought a smile to Ben's eyes.

"Let's see..." She counted on her fingers. "You put away the dishes, I'll wander around and then I'll get dressed and go home. After some coffee. But I'll make it, because you've done everything else including my laundry. How's that?"

"It's a deal." Ben came around, pulled her chair out for her and she stood up.

"Ooh." One knee gave way, and Caitlin put a hand on his chest to steady herself. The feel of Ben's heart thudding strongly beneath her palm surprised her, and she lifted her hand as though scorched. She looked up, hoping he hadn't noticed her reaction. "I think I'll be sore tomorrow. And the next day."

"And the day after that. Steady now." He held her shoulders while she got her balance, lowering his head just once to drink in the fresh scent of her clean hair. But Caitlin didn't see him do it, nor did she see the half frown on his face as he watched her limp away.

* * *

Ben was right. Caitlin felt the effects of her fence-mending experience for several days. Many times, as she busied herself over the next week with her chores on the farm and with her books in the evening, the warmth of a slow smile, the sudden flash of light in the depths of gray eyes would drift into her mind, and she'd pause, remembering their afternoon and evening together. Yet somehow, easy and companionable and relaxed as they'd been, Caitlin realized that she didn't know her neighbor any better than the day they had met.

Once, during an evening ramble with Macleary, she walked over as far as his lane. She'd considered continuing on, perhaps dropping in to see him—she convinced herself it was an ordinary neighborly thing to do—but changed her mind a hundred yards down the lane. Perhaps it was the regularly posted No Trespassing signs, perhaps it was the memory of how tenderly he'd ministered to the scratch on her arm one moment, then looked aloof and cold the next. Or perhaps it was the unwilling acknowledgment to herself of how often he'd been in her thoughts. For whatever reason, Caitlin had turned around and retraced her steps, surprised at her trepidation.

What had got into her? She hadn't felt like this since her first crush on Joel Bradstock in Grade Five. He'd been in high school and had never known she'd existed. She was now twenty-four years old, a grown woman, for Pete's sake! But somehow Ben had triggered that same feeling in her, a feeling of anticipation, of longing, of inner excitement. Good grief, she told herself, what are you thinking about? You've known this man for all of two weeks! But she knew deep down that it wasn't that simple.

To her great disappointment, Ben hadn't come over to Hollyhock Farm, either.

Once, in the barn as they finished milking, Caitlin had mentioned Ben casually to Lucas. He'd given her a shrewd glance as he straightened up, a milk pail in each gnarled hand.

"Oh, ya won't be seein' much of him."

Caitlin threw him a surprised look. "Why not? He seemed friendly enough. Helped me a lot on the fence."

"Friendly, was he? Well, well." The elderly Dutchman didn't elaborate, and Caitlin wasn't sure she should inquire further. Then Lucas turned toward the dairy with the pails. Caitlin followed him.

"He don't spend much time around here, that one. Here for a few days, gone for a month, then back again. A week or so is all he's ever stayed at one time." Caitlin was encouraged. Lucas rarely volunteered this much information.

"Then he doesn't live there all the time?" She frowned. "What about the dogs?"

"Oh, the Bensons take care of all that. Georgie Benson drives the school bus and Thelma keeps an eye on the house and feeds the dogs. You'll meet 'em soon enough. Nice folks."

Caitlin hadn't pressed further. Besides, what did it matter to her what her mysterious neighbor did? She put Ben out of her mind as well as she could and buckled down to hard reality, her business plan. As Caitlin worked out the details of her production requirements, her market strategy and her immediate and long-term cash needs, she felt more and more certain that her prospects for a loan were good. It was self-evident, she thought: a small modern cheese dairy, specializing in gourmet products for a massive sophisticated market just sixty miles away in Vancouver. What could go wrong?

Plenty, Caitlin soon found out.

"Miss Forrest, I commend you on your presentation. It's very professionally done." The young man carefully gathered the pages of her proposal and neatly lined up the edges against the polished surface of his desk.

Caitlin knew, with a sinking feeling, from the way he kept his gaze down, from the way he concentrated on the square tidiness of the pages in front of him, that the answer was no.

He looked up, the tiniest hint of sympathy in his pale blue bespectacled gaze. "But I'm afraid we have to turn you down."

"But—can you tell me why?" Caitlin sat at the edge of her chair, her brow knit with concentration, her whole body, neatly clad in a conservative navy skirt and blazer, tense. She'd hoped the low-key somber impact of the clothes she'd chosen that morning would help her in making a strong pitch for the future of Hollyhock Farm. So much for dressing for success! Luckily the bank manager hadn't seen her bounce into town in her dusty old truck, Macleary lolling happily out the passenger window.

"Well, as I said, Miss Forrest, it's a fine proposal, and I feel that you've certainly got the enthusiasm for the project. But, frankly, the bank can't go on that." He leaned forward. "It's a question of not enough experience and expertise."

She bit her lip, frowning. The man behind the desk went on. "You see, you don't have the background in farm management that we feel is essential. Your enterprise is risky, even though you've targeted your market very well. And without collateral, well…" He raised his hands, palms up, and shrugged.

"What about my farm? How about that for collateral?" Caitlin's heart sank. The last thing she wanted was to tie up her beloved Hollyhock Farm. But she knew she could make it with her gourmet cheese, and once she was in production she'd be able to pay off the bank.

"I'm afraid the bank's policy is quite firm on that, Miss Forrest." The banker's tone was gently apologetic. "So many farms have gone bankrupt in the last few years, the bank's just not interested in holding property. Your farm's only good for about half the collateral we'd need."

She stood up, thanked him and put the proposal back into her portfolio. Damn, damn, damn! Oh, well. There were other banks. One of them had to see things her way.

But by Thursday, Caitlin was thoroughly discouraged. Two other banks had had the same response as hers: no. Now she was at the local farm credit union, the last lending institution in town.

"What you've got to do, Miss Forrest, is find someone willing to take on more of a risk," said the loans manager. His brow furrowed sympathetically as he tried to come up with other financial options for her. "How about private money?"

Caitlin shook her head, miserable. Nobody she knew had the kind of money she needed. She could never go to her sister and her husband for help, not after the way they'd ridiculed her plans. Well, that was that. Perhaps everyone had been right, her little dairy at Hollyhock Farm was just another of her foolish dreams.

"What about Wade Enterprises? They're a venture capital firm, with an office here in Chilliwack. They usually invest in industrial companies, but maybe they'd consider you. It's worth a try."

Cheered, Caitlin stopped at the offices of J.B. Wade Enterprises, in the recently restored historic Hart Building in downtown Chilliwack, and dropped off her brief. When she got back to the truck, she hugged Macleary. He licked his chops with apparent embarrassment and tried to look nonchalantly out the window.

"Oh, Macleary, maybe this is it. This has got to be it! Let's keep our fingers and toes crossed." And she crossed the collie's paws firmly on the front seat before putting her key into the ignition.

Maybe it worked. Who could say? At any rate, the next morning Caitlin got a phone call confirming that the company was interested in her proposal and that Mr. Wade would like to meet with her on Monday to go over some details. Would ten-thirty in the morning be convenient? Would it! Caitlin practically whooped. Hollyhock Farm was on track!

Well before the appointed time, Caitlin sat in the plush reception area, nervously flipping through a magazine and sipping the coffee the secretary had brought her. She knew her proposal by heart and looking at it now only made things worse. The secretary had assured her that her proposal had been approved in principle or she wouldn't have been asked to come in for an interview. But Caitlin wasn't reassured. She'd worked too hard to get to this stage to take anything for granted.

She sat there, head down, while one or two people came and went from the office. Then, when she looked up next, she thought she saw a familiar back bent over the desk at the reception area. The man straightened—yes, it was Ben! What was he doing here?

Strange how she felt she'd know that broad back anywhere, the tilt of the head, the way the hair grew at the back of his neck. Only then did she realize that he was dressed very unfamiliarly to her, in a tailored, perfectly fitting dark business suit. She swallowed nervously and got to her feet.

"Ben!" She put one hand on his arm and he turned.

"Hello, Caitlin."

His voice was low, warm, and Caitlin thought he looked incredibly handsome. Somehow the formal wear suited him almost more than the jeans she had seen him in before. His eyes quickly ran down her plain linen dress, an inner smile lighting them. Caitlin realized that he'd never seen her in anything but scruffy dungarees and work shirts.

"I didn't think I'd see you here," she said, a surprised note in her voice. "Do you work here?"

"Hmm. Yes, I guess you could say that," he said, noncommittally, still smiling. His eyes were warm, but they held something else. Was it a wariness? A watchfulness? Ben straightened and took her arm. The secretary, who'd been watching this interchange with some bewilderment, finally broke in.

"Excuse me, er, Miss Forrest—"

"Yes, yes, I know," Ben interrupted, his eyes never leaving Caitlin's. "I'll take her." Ben's grip on her arm tightened, and he expertly maneuvered her around the desk and down the corridor.

"Wait, Ben, I can't go with you! I've got an appointment in a few minutes. It's extremely important—with the head honcho," Caitlin whispered loudly, very aware of the warmth of his lean, tanned fingers on her arm and of the curious glances they were receiving from passersby in the corridor.

"I know."

She looked up at him uncertainly, surprised at his brusque response. Just then they approached an open door, polished maple, with large brass handles. Ben gestured to her to enter.

Caitlin stepped inside. The room was bare except for some bookshelves along one side, a couple of upholstered chairs around a coffee table to the left and a large ebony desk with a leather chair behind it, in front of the window straight ahead. The floor was covered in a plush deep rose carpet. Caitlin looked around, startled as she heard a heavy dull click behind her.

Ben was leaning against the closed door, his arms folded on his chest. He was looking down at her, an odd look on his face, eyes intent.

"Ben . . ." Caitlin began, and stopped, unsure of how to go on. What were they doing in here? Then she raised stricken eyes to his: J. B. Wade.

"Yes, Caitlin," he said. "I am James Benjamin Wade."

Chapter Three

James Benjamin Wade! You mean—'' Caitlin heard her own voice as a whisper. She suddenly felt weak.

She sank down onto one of the upholstered chairs and closed her eyes for a few seconds, overwhelmed. Why hadn't he told her who he was right from the start?

Caitlin opened her eyes, dark with emotion, and looked at Ben. He was still leaning against the door, regarding her speculatively, arms folded across his chest. Suddenly she was very angry. What did this mean for Hollyhock Farm? For her?

"What kind of a ridiculous situation is this? Why didn't you tell me who you were?" she demanded in a low voice. Then she flushed. No wonder the secretary had been bewildered! She'd made a complete fool of herself out there. Asking Ben if he worked here! Telling him she had an important appointment—an appointment with him!

"You're angry." It was a statement.

"Of course I am! Dammit, Ben. Is this your idea of a joke? I'm afraid I don't find it the slightest bit amusing." To her horror, her voice wavered slightly. Ben strode to his desk and switched on his intercom.

"Could you bring in some coffee, Amy? Please. And I'm not to be disturbed. No calls, nothing."

In a sort of daze, Caitlin heard Ben issuing the order to his secretary. Where had she heard that tone before? He'd taken charge of her fence repairs, arranged for Lucas to do her milking for her—he was obviously used to giving orders and having them carried out. Damn! Well, she wasn't his minion, and she wasn't taking orders from him, no matter who he was!

"It's no joke, Caitlin. Nor was it ever meant to be. I'm sorry it seems to be such a shock to you—"

"Shock! That's an understatement if I—" she broke in.

But Ben continued, unperturbed. "Okay. So I'm not who you thought I was. Does it really matter?" Ben's gray eyes were earnest, with a hint of appeal in them that she'd never seen before. "I'm serious, Caitlin. What possible difference does it make?" Just then a light tap came at the big wooden doors and Ben took a tray from someone, closing the door again.

"Here." He handed her a steaming mug of coffee, just cream, the way she liked it. He'd remembered. She accepted it gratefully. Ben poured a cup for himself, black.

"Come on. It's not so bad, is it?" And he grinned at her, a familiar warm smile that Caitlin had seen before. "Once you get used to the idea?" She couldn't help wanting to smile back. Perhaps she had overreacted, maybe it was the one-quarter Irish in her, she thought—not for the first time in her life. She smiled tentatively at first.

"It was a rotten trick, Ben, and you know it. I don't know why you didn't tell me before."

"Well, to be perfectly frank, Caitlin, I don't really know the answer to that myself. Not completely. It was more of an impulse at the time. One thing led to another...." Ben leaned back in the chair beside her, clasping his hands behind his head. He frowned slightly, as though trying to make sense of the situation himself. "And then, later, well, it was damned awkward. I knew you'd be angry."

He turned toward her and grinned, all handsome charm now, and the lapels of his English worsted jacket fell back to reveal the fine texture of the silk shirt that was taut across his broad chest, the understated elegance of the perfectly knotted silk tie. She marveled again at how Ben could fill two such different roles so completely: the powerful business executive now, the enigmatic neighbor in faded jeans at Ryder Mountain.

"Of course I am. You're secretive and mistrustful and suspicious, that's why," Caitlin returned promptly. "You want to find out everything about other people before they find out anything at all about you. I'm disappointed, Ben. I thought we were friends."

He regarded her with a look of surprise, then his features softened and the light she had seen before, an intent warm light that made her tremble slightly inside, came into his eyes, and he smiled slowly. For one astonishing moment, she thought he was going to lean over and kiss her.

"Am I forgiven?"

"I don't know. Not yet. I've got to think about it for a while." But she was only half-serious. Although she didn't know why he'd done it, perhaps never would, he must have had his reasons. And she didn't really care. She trusted Benjamin Wade implicitly, although she'd never be able to explain why. It was just a feeling she had. Caitlin drained her cup and stood up. Ben got to his feet, too.

"Well," she said, businesslike again. "What does this mean to Hollyhock Farm? Do I get a loan or not?"

"Do you still want one?"

"I'm not sure," she admitted, walking over to the window, frowning.

Ben watched her walk away, her slim body held erect, unconsciously elegant.

She leaned against the window and looked down, into the busy traffic at Chilliwack's Five Corners, her lower lip held between her teeth as she studied her options. There were none.

Ordinarily she'd have scrapped the whole idea. She didn't want any favors, and she didn't like the way this had come about. She was reluctant to involve Ben in her dairy; she didn't want to owe him all that money. If she did, business ethics would preclude anything but an arm's-length relationship, and is that what she really wanted?

She cast a quick, furtive look at Ben. If she was honest, she'd have to admit she didn't, but Caitlin quickly suppressed the renegade thought. It didn't look as though she had any choice. Wade Enterprises was her only chance.

"I need the loan. For Hollyhock Farm. But I'm not happy about this, Ben. I'm not happy about you being involved." She swung around, agitation showing in her knit brow. She raised her eyes to his, turbulent blue locking with wary gray. Perhaps she imagined it, but she could feel the tension in him, too.

Ben picked up a folder from his desk, opened it and quickly scanned its contents. When he met her eyes again, Caitlin could sense the distance he'd deliberately put between them, the cool detachment.

"This is perfectly straightforward, Caitlin. As a company specializing in venture capital, Wade Enterprises is in the business of taking risks. Risks a bank might be reluctant to take on. We're always looking for ventures with the right combination of market demand, innovative strategy and entrepreneurial enthusiasm. Your proposal makes sense to us." He paused, as if cautious of how to proceed. "Our relationship, if you will, as friends and neighbors, has nothing to do with this."

She looked at him skeptically. "You mean I could have got a loan from your company even if I didn't know you?"

"If you weren't acquainted with the 'head honcho' as I think you so succinctly put it—?"

Caitlin laughed, and Ben visibly relaxed at the sound.

"Yes," he continued, "you got approval from one of my investment managers, before I even saw it. Does that make you feel better?"

"A little."

"And we'd like to look at it as an investment, not strictly a loan."

"Oh, no. It has to be a loan, Ben. I don't want a partner, and I don't want any favors. I have to do this on my own and I intend to pay back every cent I borrow, with interest." Caitlin's voice was firm. Ben looked up at her with surprise. She sounded very determined. He hesitated. "Well, if I can be frank with you . . . ?" He looked at her, one eyebrow raised in a familiar gesture.

"There's no need to pull punches with me, Ben. I know what you're going to say: no experience, no expertise, I need an investor who'll advise me on business matters. Well, the answer is no. I have to do this on my own. I don't want a partner looking over my shoulder. I don't want any kind of special deal between . . . between neighbors." She turned to the window again, considering. Then, firming her shoulders, she made her decision. It had to be done.

"How about the farm? Could you take Hollyhock Farm as collateral?"

She faced him, her distress clear in her dark blue eyes. Ben knew what it cost her to offer the farm. And should he take it? God knows, he'd wanted that land once, when the old lady had died. But now... now things were completely different. He didn't want it to even look as if he wanted that farm.

"It's not really necessary, Caitlin," he said slowly, his gray eyes serious, probing hers, feeling her agitation. "Wade Enterprises has taken far worse risks. I think we could come to some arrangement—"

"On your personal guarantee," Caitlin finished for him. "No, Ben. Take my farm as collateral or no deal. I'm not taking any special favors."

Ben regarded her in silence for a few moments, weighing her ultimatum. He couldn't push her any farther or she'd walk out. Out of this office and out of— He made his decision and stood up, offering her his hand.

"Okay. It's a deal." He smiled as he took her small hand in both of his and held it, warmly, firmly.

Caitlin flushed, partly from the excitement of finally being able to go ahead with her plans for Hollyhock Farm on her own terms, partly in response to her electric awareness of the man in front of her, an undercurrent that flashed to the surface whenever he touched her or looked deep into her eyes, as he so often did. Right now his eyes were practically twinkling.

"You drive a hard bargain, Miss Forrest. I'll enjoy doing business with a neighbor like you."

Caitlin laughed and self-consciously withdrew her hand, taking a deep breath to regain her poise. "Is that all there is to it?"

"That's it, Caitlin. You can pick up some papers from Amy on your way out. Supply us with a copy of your title to the farm, we'll draw up the documents and you can check them over with your lawyers. Then you sign on the dotted line, and the money is yours.'' He checked the date on his watch. ''You could have the money by Wednesday.''

Suddenly the enormity of her changed position struck Caitlin. Hollyhock Farm could go ahead, finally! Wait until she got going, she'd show everybody that she could make a success of it. Caitlin's eyes sparkled and her face glowed.

''Oh, Ben,'' she breathed, almost hugging herself. ''I'm so excited about this!''

He smiled to himself as she quickly walked toward the door.

At the door she turned. ''Oh, by the way. Is it still Ben? James? Benjamin? J.B.? Mr. Wade? Jim? I mean, there's so much to choose from now.'' Caitlin gave him an arch smile. Ben laughed out loud.

''Ben will be just fine.''

The next few days were a whirl of hectic activity for Caitlin. She'd hurried home, unable to believe her good fortune. But when she told Lucas the next afternoon, she hadn't missed the odd look he'd given her.

''Did he, now? A loan, eh? Well, well. More'n one way to skin a cat, they do say.'' When he hadn't added anything more, Caitlin had demanded an explanation.

''What do I mean? I guess I don't mean anything, missy. I'm gettin' too old to be surprised by much anymore.'' After a moment's thought, she decided to drop the subject. Lucas seemed particularly wary on the subject of their mutual neighbor.

But as far as the dairy went, Lucas went from being one of its biggest detractors to one of its biggest boosters. He spent many hours that probably would have been better spent tending to chores on his own farm, sitting in her grandmother's old rocking chair on the veranda, liberally dispensing advice.

Caitlin was glad of his company and the activity and the trips to and from Chilliwack and Vancouver to visit suppliers and arrange for licenses from the various authorities, because she hadn't seen Ben since her trip to his office. And she missed him. The one time she'd had the courage to take a turn down his lane on her way back from town, she'd been disappointed to find that he wasn't there. George Benson, the caretaker, had been there feeding the dogs and said he didn't know when Ben would be back, never did.

The news had jarred her. In fact, the strength of her disappointment shocked her.

"Caitlin Emily Forrest, you're being ridiculous!" she told herself out loud as she bumped and lurched over the potted gravel road the remaining distance home in the old truck. Macleary's nails scratched the worn seat as he desperately tried to keep both his position and his dignity. He'd long ago stopped responding to Caitlin's confessions, except for a sympathetic whine or cocked ear when she actually looked at him. She didn't now, just glared at the road out the cracked windshield.

"You'd better watch out, my girl," she went on, "before you end up making a big fool out of yourself. Where's your common sense? You don't know a thing about the man, didn't even know his last name until last week! And now you owe him money, too. Big money. You've got a dairy to start up and make pay because he's got a mortgage on your farm." She ground the gears on the old truck down to second and turned into her lane. Common sense didn't seem as comforting as it once had.

Caitlin threw herself into her plans with renewed energy. She was so immersed in her research that she went to bed each night exhausted, dreaming of enzymes and bacteria and package designs and cows, cows, cows yielding floods of milk. Floods of milk that had to be turned into vats and vats of cheese. Sometimes Caitlin awoke in a cold sweat, unsure of herself, wondering if perhaps she'd tackled something bigger than she really wanted to handle.

And she felt alone, too. The peace and satisfaction she felt during the day with just Macleary and the cows and perhaps the occasional visitor, deserted her at night when she felt the huge black bulk of Ryder Mountain at her back, breathing silently over her shoulder, the sigh of the wind at her bedroom curtains, the far-off rugg-rugg of frogs at Flat Pond. Was this really what she wanted—a life alone at Hollyhock Farm?

But there was no going back, and Caitlin, pragmatist that she was, always dismissed her fears in the morning.

A week before her launch, Caitlin wrote out a check for Larry Sanderson, a tall young man with sandy hair and freckles who'd installed her new milking parlor.

"Let's see, now... when do you expect the steam jacket for the yogurt incubator to get here?" Caitlin queried.

"Supplier said about the middle of next week, maybe sooner."

"Okay. Here you go, Larry." She ripped off the check and handed it to him with a smile. "Don't spend it all in one place." She'd never had that much money in a bank account before. Thank goodness Wade Enterprises had backed her.

That made her think of Ben again, and Caitlin frowned slightly. Wasn't he the slightest bit interested in what was happening with his money, her loan—his investment as he'd wanted to call it? Still, she'd told him she wanted to do it all on her own, and it looked as though Ben were letting her do just that.

Larry didn't even look at the check, just folded it up and stuck it into his shirt pocket. He grinned at her.

"How about you and me spend some of this? There's a dance at the Elk River Community Hall on Saturday. I'd love to show up with the best looking gal in the valley."

Caitlin shook her head. Larry was unabashed. This wasn't the first time she'd turned him down. It seemed he intended to keep on trying.

"Sorry, Larry. There are just too many details for me to clear up now, with the grand opening so soon." She bit her lip. "Think everything will be ready on time?"

He patted her hand. "If Larry Sanderson says it'll be ready, it will be. But, hey, just don't forget what they say about all work and no play?" He stood up and settled his cap on his head. "See ya later."

Larry's confidence in himself was well placed. On Friday, half an hour before anyone was due to arrive, Caitlin quickly checked everything again. The dairy looked lovely, with red-and-white checkered cloths on all the serving tables. The Women's Institute ladies, smartly turned out in crisp red-and-white gingham aprons, were readying trays of hors d'oeuvres and sweets, and all the flowers, mostly roses and hollyhocks and daisies from the farm, looked fresh and lovely on the tables and showcases. Everything looked perfect. Now, Caitlin thought, fingers crossed, if only I get some favorable publicity and maybe even an order or two.

Caitlin had dressed carefully in elegant red pumps and a navy-and-red dress, knowing intuitively that her image was almost as important as her product at this stage. She wanted to dispel any notion that might be harbored by the press or potential buyers that Hollyhock Farm was a two-bit mom-and-pop operation in the backwoods of Ryder Mountain. If she was going to make her dairy a success and pay back the big loan she owed Wade Enterprises, she not only had to know what she was doing, she had to look like she knew what she was doing.

Finally the great moment arrived, and neighbors began to gather. Everyone was in a festive mood, many had brought their children, and a few had even brought their dogs. Macleary seemed torn between the dignity he seemed to know the occasion required—Caitlin had given him a good brushing only that morning—and the fun that could be had racing around with the Erskine's hound and chasing sticks for the boys down in the orchard. After one or two guilty looks at Caitlin, he followed his heart and slunk down to the orchard.

Within an hour, the dairy was full of visitors, and family groups were strolling about the grounds. Caitlin was thrilled. She had wanted the local community's approval, and with the full turnout, she knew she had it.

Well, not quite full turnout. Caitlin's brow clouded slightly and her smile seemed a trifle frozen just for an instant, as she answered questions for the local reporter, a pimply lad who seemed tangled up in his camera equipment and full of rather dull questions. Caitlin answered them patiently, all the time scanning the crowd for one familiar tall figure.

She paused by one of the big old trees a couple of hours later and watched the crowd. The Laflamme brothers had produced their fiddles and set up under the large maples by the dairy. A few couples were dancing on the lawn, there was a great deal of laughter, and small children were climbing about on the piles of stones Caitlin had so painstakingly carried from the garden. It seemed so long ago, had it really been only a month and a half?

Suddenly Caitlin felt very tired, and she realized for the first time what a very long day it had been. She'd been up at dawn, as usual, milking. Then Caitlin felt a presence behind her, a prickling sensation at the back of her neck, a flutter in her pulse, and she whirled around.

"Hello, Caitlin."

"Ben!" Her weariness evaporated and her gladness showed in her wide smile and happy eyes. "Where have you been? I thought you might not come."

He didn't answer immediately, just stood in front of her, looking at her slowly, taking in every detail.

"Did you miss me?" Ben asked.

His voice was very low, dark velvet, and the feel of it swept over her like a caress in the half dusk. She shivered.

"I—" She looked up at him, her feeling naked in her eyes. "Yes," she whispered. "I did." Then she caught herself and stepped back.

"You look very happy, Caitlin," Ben said finally.

The moment of their meeting had passed, the moment when her heart had lurched crazily. Thank goodness!

"I am, Ben." She stepped forward and grasped his hands. "Oh, I am. Everything is going so well. All the neighbors came, food brokers came, critics, wholesalers, everybody—" Her face changed, her intensity fractured. "Except you."

"And did you want me to be here?" His words were teasing, and he smiled a little.

"Of course I did! After all, I wouldn't have been able to do any of this if you hadn't loaned me money." She waved one hand around the orchard, taking in the dairy, the refurbished barn. She was still holding his hand, and now she realized it and released it, stepping back.

"Wade Enterprises, Caitlin, not me."

"Oh, pooh! That's just a technicality and we both know it. You believed in me, you thought I could do it." She looked up at him, caught his serious gaze, with the tiny crinkles of laughter around the cool gray eyes. God, how she'd missed him! She hadn't even known how much until now.

"Oh, I don't know, Caitlin. I think you would have found a way to do it anyway. Somehow. You've got plenty of grit."

"Oh, Ben!" She took his hands again, impulsively, bringing them together with hers. "Come on. Let me show you everything I've done."

For a moment longer he stood smiling down at her, holding her hands firmly in his, and she felt again the enormous pull that seemed to bind them together, seemed to bind her to him at least. It was scary. She'd never felt anything like it before.

Just then she became aware of a woman calling his name. Surprised, she wrenched her eyes from Ben's and looked past his shoulder. A tall blonde was approaching, two champagne glasses in her hands. She was smartly dressed in a pale green suit, superbly tailored but very feminine.

"Oh, there you are, Ben."

Caitlin dropped Ben's hands as if they were hot potatoes.

The woman positioned herself very close to Ben. "I'd wondered where you'd wandered off to." She handed Ben a glass and raised her eyebrows at Caitlin, giving her a curious look.

"Jennifer, I'd like you to meet Caitlin Forrest." He turned to the older woman. "Miss Forrest is the proprietor of Hollyhock Farm. And Caitlin, this is Jennifer Brownlee, senior vice president of Wade Enterprises and my right-hand man—or rather—woman."

Chapter Four

Had she imagined it, or had Ben favored Jennifer Brownlee with a special smile when he'd emphasized "woman"? Her stomach tightened. But then good manners took over and she extended her hand, smiling politely. Jennifer laughed, a low, musical sound, and took Caitlin's hand in a brief handclasp.

"Oh, yes! The cheese lady you've told me so much about," she murmured, with a slanted look up at Ben. "What a pleasure."

"I was just about to show Mr. Wade the improvements in the dairy," Caitlin said smoothly. "Would you care to join us?"

"Oh, heavens, no. Dairies are hardly—" she grimaced at Ben, who gave her a swift smile "—my area of expertise, are they, Ben? No. I think I might have a word with that nice little man in real estate, was it Mr. Chadwick? The one over there in the—dear me, is that really an argyle vest?" Jennifer Brownlee deposited her empty glass regally in Ben's hand and moved purposefully across the grass without a backward glance, leaving in her wake a cloud of expensive scent.

Expensive or not, Caitlin thought, wrinkling her nose, she preferred the smell of the barn any day. Was this Ben's kind of woman—urbane, elegant, well turned out? The kind who always made her feel all elbows and knees and thirteen years old again?

Ben turned from his amused glance after Jennifer to Caitlin, just catching her fleeting look of disdain. He laughed out loud.

"I take it you're not impressed with our Miss Brownlee? I assure you her manner hides a razor-sharp brain."

I'll bet it does! Caitlin thought. So she wasn't married, either. Senior vice president. Humph!

"I expect I won't be seeing much of her, anyway," she said airily. "As she said, barns are not her strong suit. So my opinion is rather irrelevant, isn't it?" Caitlin schooled her features carefully, determined to present a smooth facade to Ben. What did she care about Jennifer Brownlee? Or Benjamin Wade for that matter? He looked down at her, smiling, an odd glint in his eyes.

"On the contrary. Jennifer is in the process of moving up to the valley. She'll be taking over the Chilliwack office. After I've groomed her a little more." Caitlin shot him a sharp glance.

He grinned. "It wouldn't do to have her offending all our agricultural clients with her opinion of barns, would it?"

She bit back the reply that was ready on the tip of her tongue and smiled sweetly. "Speaking of barns, shall we go?"

Ben took her arm and they walked slowly back through the orchard. Caitlin pointed out the modern features of the milking parlor, took him through the dairy, showed him the shiny stainless steel cheese and yogurt vats, the modern refrigeration facilities, and finally took him into the showroom, were a few hardy souls still lingered over the canapé trays. Ben took in everything, nodding here, asking a pointed question there.

Finally they emerged outside again. Ben stood in front of her, glanced quickly at his watch, then folded his arms and looked down at her.

"Well?" Caitlin waited expectantly.

"Well, what?"

"Well. What do you think of it? You haven't said a word. Do you like it?" Caitlin was beside herself. The fact that Ben had nodded gravely and asked the right questions had pleased her, but he hadn't ventured an opinion at all.

"I like it."

"That's all?" She was astonished.

"No," he said slowly, with an enigmatic smile that warmed Caitlin's blood. "That's not all. But if you mean the dairy, I like it. I think you've done a fine job in a few weeks, considering what you started with. And if your product and marketing are as good as your preparation, I expect Hollyhock Dairy to be a great success."

"Oh, Ben," she said, smiling radiantly up at him, her eyes sparkling. "Do you mean it? Do you really think it's going to go?"

"You've made a great start."

Caitlin was so happy she nearly threw her arms around him. Somehow his opinion was vital to her, vital to her success as she saw it. Then he glanced at his watch again, and Caitlin curbed her impulse, remembering Jennifer.

"Well, nice to see you doing so well, Caitlin. Keep up the good work." He began walking toward the driveway, and she walked along with him. He kept looking over the heads of the people still around them. Then he waved.

"Yoo-hoo!" Jennifer made her way over, stepping care-fully across the lawn in her high-heeled sandals.

The two women exchanged polite goodbyes and Ben handed Jennifer into his car, a dark blue Jaguar, all leather and polished wood inside. Expensive car, expensive woman.

Caitlin felt strangely bereft, after the euphoria of a mo-ment ago. Whatever could she have been thinking about? Imagining? Fantasizing about? The car and the woman in it went together with a certain kind of man. J.B. Wade. This was the real Ben, then, not the neighbor in faded jeans she'd met in her garden. The man who'd helped fix her fence.

"Caitlin?" Some of her pain must have shown, because he stopped in front of her before opening the driver's door, a frown on his face.

Unwilling to meet his gaze, Caitlin studied his shirt front, immediately in front of her eyes, with a sense of detach-ment. It was rather nice, with pearly brown buttons, and the fabric looked like pima cotton. She resisted the sudden im-pulse she had to stroke its surface lightly with her fingers, to feel its satin smoothness and the warmth of the living, breathing man underneath. Then Ben tilted up her chin with one hand and she trembled slightly.

For a long moment serious gray eyes looked deep into gentian blue ones. Her eyes were shimmering suspiciously in the dim light. His darkened, and he bent infinitesimally closer to her. Her midriff tightened just under her ribs, and her breath caught in her throat. My Lord, he can't be going to kiss me! Not right here, not now!

The world contracted to just the two of them for the briefest instant, then burst.

"Chin up, Caitlin. You're doing a great job." And with that he released her and got into the car. She watched him leave with Jennifer, and a little part of her, deep inside, a little part she'd never really known was there, hurt in a way she'd never felt before.

The next ten days were filled with activity Caitlin welcomed, because when her mind and body were occupied, she could forget her wild speculations about Ben and his senior vice president. She had heard from Lucas—heaven knows how he came by the latest gossip, but he always did—that Miss Brownlee had taken up residence next door. Whether temporarily or permanently, Caitlin didn't know and told herself she didn't care.

The van Holst's eldest daughter, Willie, had expressed a desire to learn the dairy business. With her help, Caitlin buried herself in work: setting milk to clabber in the big vats, testing various combinations of herbs from her garden to combine with the soft spreadable cheese and sending out samples to potential customers.

This morning, Willie, a sturdy blond woman with her short hair tied up in a polka-dot handkerchief was in the dairy with Caitlin. She carried in a box of plastic containers and fitted them onto the machine that filled them.

"Here it comes!" Caitlin turned on the spigot, and the bright red containers came off behind the machine, filled and sealed with lids designed by a local artist, featuring a line drawing of the homestead, with hollyhocks in bloom, and the words, Hollyhock Farm Yogurt.

Caitlin never got over the thrill. It was a reality! Her grandmother's rocky backwoods farm had become a busy little cottage dairy, and she knew how proud of her Grandma Bevan would have been. She took off her white cotton overalls, revealing a white blouse and green culottes, and ran a comb through her tangled hair. Presto! She was ready to make deliveries.

Caitlin drove the rented refrigerator van carefully over the potholed mountain road. In the back were a couple of cases of yogurt she was taking to a buyer at Chilliwack's farmers' market.

She passed Ben's lane. She hadn't seen him since her grand opening, but Lucas had kept her up on the local gossip. Of course Lucas could be wrong, she thought, frowning in concentration as she maneuvered the van around a particularly nasty-looking bump. Perhaps Ben wasn't there at all. Lucas had said that he rarely stayed at Ryder Mountain for long. But surely he wouldn't have left Jennifer on her own. She hardly seemed the rustic type. Were they lovers? Did she care?

Don't be a ninny, Caitlin warned herself. Ben Wade was a good-looking, virile man, a man who would be used to plenty of attention from women. Plus he was rich, powerful, successful. A dynamite combination. Jennifer would be only the latest in what was probably a very long line.

"Ha! And you're turning out to be just as susceptible, my girl," she muttered to herself. But it wasn't J. B. Wade, venture capitalist, she was drawn to, she told herself. It was Ben, her vanished taciturn neighbor with the calm gray eyes.

Caitlin sighed, conscious of a sadness that had seeped into her lately. You silly fool, she thought angrily, you've got a crush on him, just like any schoolgirl. Then she squared her shoulders. Well, there was no point in mooning over J. Benjamin Wade. She was going to do something about it.

When Caitlin got home that evening, Willie had gone home for the day and the cows were waiting for her at the barn door.

"Move along there, Martha," she said affectionately to her favorite, a very pregnant matron who was always the last to enter. Caitlin liked the time spent in the barn filled with the scent of hay and feed grains and fragrant with the cows' grassy breath. It was an oasis of femininity, of maternity, of peace and contentment.

She put the cows through the milking parlor in groups. Each cow munched on feed concentrates, rich with extra protein and molasses, while they were milked. By now, thanks to Lucas's coaching, the procedure of cleansing udders, snapping on milking equipment, cleaning filters and hoses, was second nature to Caitlin, and she could finish up the milking, morning and evening, in just over an hour. But it was a tedious chore, and now that she was so busy in the dairy, she knew she'd have to hire someone soon to help her with the barn work. She'd have to ease off on the killing pace she'd set herself or she'd end up sick, and where would that leave Hollyhock Farm?

As the cows settled down to their hay, Caitlin checked each one for signs of illness or injuries the way Lucas had shown her. Sometimes one picked up a stone in her foot and began limping, he'd said, sometimes barbed wire snagged the neck or ears of a greedy cow reaching for the grass in the next meadow, always greener.

Today there were no injuries. Martha looked awfully pregnant to Caitlin's inexperienced eye, but Lucas had told her not to worry.

"Once in a while you might get a heifer what might get in a little trouble with her first calf," Lucas had explained. "But a jersey usually drops her calf easy as a mule deer." And he'd told her it was best to let them calve in the open field. The grass was clean and soft and there weren't the dangerous microbes that could build up in a barn and cause trouble for the new mother or young calf.

Caitlin eyed Martha critically. Trouble was, Caitlin wasn't sure when Martha'd been bred. Her grandmother hadn't kept very good records, and although two cows had calved successfully since Caitlin's arrival—both surprises—she was keeping an eye on Martha. She didn't want anything to go wrong for her favorite.

Caitlin quickly finished her solitary supper in the farmhouse kitchen, with only the voice of the Canadian Broadcasting Corporation for company. She was getting into a rut, she knew that. Larry Sanderson had warned her. Caitlin rinsed her plate, then thumbed through the local phone book for his number.

"Larry?" She could tell he was pleased to hear from her. She brightened. Maybe this wouldn't be as hard as she'd thought.

"What's up, Caitlin?"

"This is kind of hard to say, Larry. But—well, I've been thinking. I know I turned you down quite a few times, but I've—I've changed my mind. I'd like to meet some more people up here. And I thought maybe you could introduce me around. After all, you know everybody." There, she'd done it.

"Just a minute. Let me get this straight." Caitlin could practically see Larry's grin. "Are you asking me for a date?"

"I guess you could call it that. The trouble is, I don't know where to ask you—on a date, as you put it."

"No problem. There's another country dance comin' up on Saturday. At Cultus Lake. How 'bout that for starters?"

Caitlin smiled as she hung up. There's no way she felt the slightest bit romantic about Larry Sanderson, and she knew he knew that, too. But she needed to get out more, and Larry seemed happy to oblige.

Late that night—or perhaps it wasn't so late, Caitlin wasn't sure because she'd awoken from a deep sleep she'd fallen into, fully clothed on the sofa—the phone rang. Caitlin jumped, startled. Who could that be? She sat up sleepily and reached for the receiver. Probably her mother. Her parents had become cautiously optimistic about her new venture since the orders had begun rolling in.

"Hello?" Caitlin's voice was still husky from sleep. There was a silence.

"Caitlin?" It was Ben. He sounded slightly puzzled.

"Ben! What are you doing calling at this hour?" She was pleased. He'd never phoned her before.

"I didn't wake you, did I?" There was a pause, then she heard the quiet amusement in his voice. "It's all of half past nine."

Caitlin yawned hugely, deliciously. "Oh, sorry, Ben. Yes. I'm afraid I fell asleep here in the living room."

"You're working too hard."

"Hmm. Yeah, you're probably right." Caitlin still was a little muzzy. "Where are you, Ben? You sound a long way away."

"I'm in Vancouver. But I'm coming up in a couple of days. That's what—"

"You mean you're not next door? I thought you'd be keeping Jennifer amused?" Caitlin could have bitten her tongue. It was one thing to speculate in private, quite another to sarcastically inquire about something that was none of her business. There was a brief silence on the other end.

"No. I'm not. Actually, Jennifer doesn't need me to amuse her, she's quite good at amusing herself, believe it or not."

He wasn't angry. Caitlin heaved a sigh of relief. "I'm sorry, Ben. Really. It's none of my business. What can I do for you?" She was determined to put the conversation back on a more businesslike footing. She was wide-awake now.

"I called to ask if you were free Saturday evening. I'd like to take you out."

Caitlin was shocked. This was the last thing she'd expected. "You mean—on a date?" She unconsciously echoed Larry's words earlier. Ben laughed, a warm rich sound that Caitlin responded to with a grin.

"Well, yes, actually. That was the idea. What do you think?"

"Oh, Ben, I'd love—" She was just about to accept impulsively, genuine pleasure in her voice, when she suddenly remembered her arrangements with Larry. "I—I'll have to say no, Ben, I'm afraid. I've got something arranged for Saturday. Sorry."

Caitlin's disappointment in having to turn Ben down was tempered with her relief in at least having a good excuse. This wasn't, couldn't be, just a simple garden-variety date. She owed Benjamin Wade a lot of money, he had a live-in lady next door—so Lucas had hinted—and he held a mortgage on her farm. There were plenty of good reasons not to start dating Benjamin Wade.

"I see." Ben's voice was cooler, held that note of reserve that she'd always sensed in him. "Hmm. Well, perhaps another time."

"Yes." Caitlin hesitated. She wanted to say something, anything, to lessen the distance she sensed from Ben, but she didn't know what to say. Perhaps it was best this way. Neighbors, perhaps friends in a fashion, but that was all they could be.

After she hung up, Caitlin checked the doors and made her way sleepily to her bedroom, discarding clothing as she went. Gee, nothing for weeks, then two offers in one evening. Of course, she admitted, yawning, she'd arranged one of them herself. Caitlin smiled. What was that saying that it never rains, but it pours?

* * *

Caitlin had cause to remember that expression on Saturday morning when she turned the cows out after morning milking. It was a gloomy day, the dark rain clouds hovering sulkily over the peak of Ryder Mountain, low drifts caught in the trees of the high valleys.

As she looked around the misty gray-green landscape of her beloved Hollyhock Farm, she wondered again about the anonymous bidder who'd wanted the farm after her grandmother had died. It wasn't the sort of place an ordinary farmer would want. Too rocky, too isolated, too marginal, too small.

In fact, at barely thirty acres, Hollyhock shouldn't even be a farm. Its highest pastures butted onto rugged crown land on Ryder Mountain. The van Holsts were on the other side of the road, lower down the valley, on more arable soil. She was the end of the line, and the public road ended just past the lane to Hollyhock Farm, near Flat Pond. Benjamin Wade was her only neighbor to the north.

Caitlin shrugged and turned into the dairy. Well, there wasn't much point in thinking about it. She hadn't sold, and now she never would.

By late afternoon, the clouds were building up, and what's more, Caitlin decided Martha's confinement was imminent. When she'd gone out to open the gates for the jerseys' return to the barn that evening, she'd found Martha waiting for her at the last gate, lowing softly.

"I think we'd better get you somewhere safe," she said to the fawn-colored animal. Martha swung her head heavily toward Caitlin and licked her own wet nose with a long black tongue. Caitlin sensed the appeal in the liquid brown eyes. She had no trouble getting the cow back to the barn. Martha followed heavily at her shoulder, swollen udder rubbing against her hind legs as she walked.

"Udder distended, concave at hips, restlessness..." Caitlin mentally ticked off Martha's symptoms against the list of signs of approaching labor she'd read about in an old veterinary manual she'd found in her grandmother's library. It looked as though Martha had them all. So much for her evening out.

"Larry?" Caitlin rang Larry Sanderson up as soon as she'd seen Martha safely into a roomy box stall well littered with fresh straw. "I'm afraid I have to cancel. Martha's going to have her calf tonight.... Yeah, I'm sorry, too."

It was a good thing Larry was a country boy, she thought, smiling ruefully as she hung up. How many of her Vancouver dates would have been as understanding about being bumped for a pregnant cow?

As the evening wore on, Caitlin had to admit that she wasn't all that sorry she'd missed the dance. The wind sweeping down the mountain made the old house creak and groan, but in a friendly way, as though reassuring Caitlin that it had survived many such storms and would survive many more.

She made herself a thick tomato-and-cheese sandwich liberally smeared with mustard and packed up a vacuum bottle of hot chocolate and a tin of homemade shortbread cookies. Who knew how long a vigil she might have? She walked down to the barn, accompanied by Macleary, glad of the extra sweater she'd pulled on at the last moment under the jacket. It was cold for late July. And by the look of the sky, this was no passing blow.

A couple of hours later Caitlin looked up from her book and wondered idly if there was such a thing as false labor with cows, and if not, just how long did it take for a calf to be born? Was Martha in trouble? How did you tell?

All the books she'd consulted—and she'd brought her entire stock of volumes relating to veterinary medicine to the barn with her—mentioned problems that might occur a little further along, when the calf had started to be born. She'd learned that headfirst was normal and that Martha might lie down at the last moment or have it standing up. What else?

Caitlin decided the best plan was to take her main cues from Martha herself. The jersey seemed nonchalant about the whole process. Between pushing, she calmly chewed her cud, occasionally getting up to take a drink of water. Caitlin found that reassuring.

The wind howled outside the barn, rattling some loose shingles, but it was snug and warm inside. She could hear the rain pelting down on the roof, hard as gravel in the driving fury of the wind. Far off she heard the sudden muffled crack of thunder. Macleary was making interminable rounds of the barn, alternately listening, then desperately scratching and digging in the corners for mice. Most of the cows were lying down, chewing their cuds, making low contented sounds in their throats from time to time, their eyes luminous in the lamplight.

What was that? Caitlin stiffened, listening. Macleary had heard it, too, and stood, one paw raised, ears cocked, in the classic pose of the bird dog. Then he let out a low growl and raced for the door. Caitlin's heart lurched. She was all alone out here. It could be anybody. Or anything.

"Caitlin? Anybody here?"

"Ben! Oh, my goodness, you scared me half to death sneaking in like that." She got to her feet and rushed over to the barn door. Ben was just pushing it closed behind him, against the wind. He grinned down at her, breathing hard, then reached up to run his fingers through his wet hair.

"Sneaking in? Is that what you call it?" Ben raised a forearm to wipe the rain from his face.

Now that he was in the circle of the lamplight, she could see that he was drenched. Caitlin didn't know what to say, she was just so glad to see him.

"What are you doing here, anyway?" She took him by the arm. "Come on over where it's warmer."

"I saw the lights. Thought somebody must be down here—probably you." He took in Martha's situation at a glance. "This looks very cosy. Is this what you meant by a previous arrangement?" He looked down at her, eyes twinkling.

For a moment she was nonplussed, then she remembered her excuse for not going out with him. "No. Actually I had to beg off with Larry Sanderson over this." She laughed but didn't miss the narrowing of his eyes at her mention of Sanderson. He took off his jacket and hung it on a convenient nail. Underneath he was wearing an Aran sweater, and it looked fairly dry.

"Know anything about calving?"

Ben gave her a sharp glance, then looked at Martha for a moment thoughtfully. "I'm afraid not. You?"

"Not much." She looked at him ruefully, then began to laugh. "Some farmer I am, eh?"

"Have you called the vet?"

"No. So far she seems to know what she's doing."

Ben smiled. "Glad one of us does." He walked over to the little nest in the straw she'd built for herself and bent to pick up the vacuum bottle. "Anything in this flask?"

Martha turned to look at him once, then cast a baleful eye at Caitlin as if to ask what in the world a man was doing in here.

"Sit down, sit down." Ben gestured at the straw and then, when Caitlin had taken her place again, he lowered himself beside her, nudging at a bale of straw until he could lean against it comfortably. He poured out a cup of hot chocolate and warmed his fingers around it, long legs stretched out in front of him.

"Cookie?"

Ben looked down at the tin she held out. "Hmm. Thanks." He took one and munched it solemnly, then turned to catch her eye. "Pleasant way to spend a Saturday evening, don't you think?" he drawled.

Caitlin pealed with laughter, then immediately clapped her hand over her mouth as she realized she was disturbing the cows. They'd all stopped chewing and had swung their heads around to look at her and Ben.

"Got any more of these?" He reached for another cookie. "They're very good. I suppose you made them yourself." She nodded; he smiled. Just then Martha began straining again, this time for several minutes.

"Oh, Ben," Caitlin whispered. "Do you think she's having it now?"

"I don't know. She seems to know what she's doing, doesn't she?" Caitlin had to agree. The cow didn't seem in any distress, didn't seem inordinately tired—signs the books had said to watch for. Martha walked around the stall a bit, then stopped and strained again. Caitlin could see a clear sac protruding from behind the cow. As she strained, the sac got larger. Then Martha relaxed and began chewing again, seemingly unconcerned.

"This looks like it could take some time," Ben whispered, his breath warm in her ear.

Caitlin shivered slightly.

"Cold?"

"No. Just—just excited, I guess," she whispered. "I've never seen anything born before."

"Why are we whispering?" he whispered.

Caitlin giggled softly. "I don't know." Just then the sky outside lit up and there was a loud crack of thunder. Caitlin shuddered involuntarily and Ben put his arm around her. For a moment she closed her eyes and leaned against him. He felt so warm and solid and safe, and she felt so comfortable and . . . and happy, having Ben in the barn with her like this.

For a few moments they sat like that, quietly nestled into the straw, listening to the lash of the wind and rain outside and the muffled movements of the animals inside. Even Macleary had given up his mad pursuit of vermin and was sound asleep on a bale of straw.

It must be getting late, Caitlin thought, reluctant to move even to look at her watch. Suddenly she became very aware of the warmth of Ben's breath on her cheek. He had turned to her and brushed her temple lightly with his lips. Now she could feel him watching her, but she kept her eyes downcast.

"Caitlin?" His voice was low.

She glanced quickly up at him, then down again. She couldn't look at him, couldn't hold those eyes without drowning in them, without giving away everything she was feeling at this moment. Ben pulled her tighter against him with one arm, and she could feel the solid heat of his chest, smell the damp wool of his sweater—a thoroughly male scent—and feel the deep strong thud of his heart beneath her cheek. For an instant she felt panic, then Ben brought his other arm around so he was holding her closely, the top of her head tucked under his chin. She felt him sigh, and his arms tightened for a fraction of a second. Then he released her as quietly and easily as he'd embraced her.

Martha gave a low, long groan and Caitlin instantly sat up.

"Ben!" She stood and went over to the cow's head, stroking her muzzle gently as Martha half closed her eyes and concentrated, turned inward to the eternal rhythms of her body. She moaned again and pushed.

"I think we're getting closer," Ben said, moving around to the back of the cow.

Martha moved her hind legs restlessly, tail rigid, then re-laxed. Now they could see the calf's forefeet and nose, just like the books had said. Caitlin was suddenly seized with an inexpressible excitement. The forever-old, ever-new miracle of birth was unfolding before them.

Martha turned in her stall once or twice, examining the straw behind her, then lay down again. This time she looked as though she were all business. Ben and Caitlin stood watching, silent, hand in hand, as the cow pushed once, twice, and then the calf was there, all shiny and limp in the straw.

"Do you think we should do anything? It's alive, isn't it?" Caitlin whispered to Ben, suddenly horrified that something might be wrong with the calf. Just then the limbs moved spasmodically, and Caitlin took a deep breath. She stepped forward to clear the tiny creature's nose and mouth with a cloth.

Martha had swung her head around and was regarding the goings-on behind her with an expression of surprise. Then she heaved to her feet and came around to see things for herself. Immediately the rough tongue began licking and massaging, bringing rough whorls of hair up on the tiny body. By now the little calf, a heifer, Caitlin noted with sat-isfaction, was breathing easily and reached up its tiny black nose to its mother's. Martha gave it a generous lick.

"Looks like mother and daughter will be just fine," Ben said, breaking the silence and looking over to Caitlin with a broad grin. He squeezed her hand. "I'm glad I found you here tonight. I feel very privileged."

Caitlin gave him a shy smile. "Me, too." She let go of Ben's hand—when had she reached for it?—and bent down to gather up her things. Ben took down his wet jacket and shrugged it on.

"Here, let me carry that." He took up her rucksack easily in one hand and slung it over his shoulder. They made their way to the barn door, still caught up in the magic of the birth they'd just witnessed.

As they opened the door, there was suddenly another flash of lightning and a loud clap of thunder above them, a little to the east. The storm seemed to be moving on, but the rain was still lashing down in a fury outside.

"We'll have to run for it," Ben shouted above the wind. "Okay?"

After Caitlin nodded, Ben pulled her collar up around her ears. He gripped her hand. "One, two, three—go!"

And they raced through the dark soggy barnyard, leaping over hummocks and stopping just once, to open the gate. Then they ran again, around the corner of the dairy, across the pavement by the garage and up the steps of the veranda. They stopped, both panting, both streaming with water.

"Oh, Ben," Caitlin said weakly, putting her hand on his arm for support. She was laughing and so was he, all the tension in the barn dissipated in their mad dash through the storm.

Then Ben stopped laughing. He dropped the rucksack and his arms went around her. She looked up, startled, and another flash of lightning lit up the landscape, showing her his face, eyes dark with intent in the split second of brilliance. Slowly he lowered his mouth to hers, raising his hands to push his fingers through her wet hair on either side of her face. He kissed her warmly, tenderly, deeply, the taste of his lips a focus of heat and comfort in the storm raging around them.

She trembled at the wave of feeling that surged over her. And then, because it was as natural to her as breathing, she reached her hands up to his wet shoulders, fingers curling under the hair on his collar, and pulled him closer. Closer, closer—she couldn't get close enough to him. Her lips softened and moved under his, responding instinctively to the age-old call of the blood.

She sensed rather than heard Ben's low groan as he felt her yield to him, and with a sudden fierceness he dropped his hands from her hair and enclosed her, hard, in his arms. She clung to him. His lips demanded more as they sought a deep response from Caitlin, and she opened her mouth to him and gave freely, with a hunger that matched his. Her pulse hammered in her ears, sang in her veins, leaped to meet the rhythm of his. Her uninhibited response shook her. She had never felt like this—ever—before.

Then suddenly he pulled back. She looked at him, her face pale in the darkness of the veranda, her whole body trembling. He bent and kissed her chin and nose and forehead, wet with rain. He rubbed his cheek against hers, gently, rough against smooth.

"Caitlin. Oh, Caitlin, I—" he murmured, then stopped himself, his voice husky with restraint. Ben pulled her into his arms again and held her tightly for a moment, his face buried in her neck, as though he could never let her go. Then he did, abruptly.

"You're soaking, Caitlin. You'd better get some dry things on or you'll catch something." His voice was very low, but normal sounding now. It even held a note of slight amusement.

Catch something? Caitlin thought as she followed him through the door. I think I already have.

Chapter Five

By the time Caitlin had stripped off her wet clothes, toweled her hair and changed into some dry jeans and a fleecy top, she'd had time to think about what had happened on the veranda. If, indeed, anything had.

After all, she told herself, wincing as she yanked a comb through her damp hair, it was just a kiss. Big deal! If you'd gone out with Larry tonight like you'd planned, he probably would have kissed you good-night. But would a kiss from Larry have shaken her like this?

She examined her face critically in the mirror. Her eyes were a little brighter than normal, and her cheeks had a high color, but otherwise she looked just the same. Caitlin touched one finger gingerly to her lips. She felt that they should feel changed, still soft with Ben's kisses. But they looked perfectly normal.

"Where do you keep the coffee?" Ben called through the closed door to her bedroom.

"The yellow canister by the fridge," she called back. She could hear him knocking about in the kitchen as he hunted for her coffeepot. Caitlin hopped around on first one leg, then the other, as she pulled on some woolly socks. Her feet felt cold as ice. She heard the loud whir of her coffee grinder.

At the entrance to the kitchen, Caitlin paused for a moment, her hand on the dark wood frame. Ben was concentrating on pouring the boiling water evenly into her drip coffee filter. He looked incredibly handsome, tall in his creamy sweater and faded jeans, his dark hair in disarray from running his fingers through it. He'd hung his wet jacket on a hook behind the wood stove.

"I thought you might like something hot," he said, not interrupting his study of the stream of hot water for an instant. He'd known she was there, silent as she was on stocking feet.

"Thanks. I would." Caitlin took out her cream and sugar set, delft blue that matched the paint on the old wood dresser against one wall. Then she opened the fridge door to get the cream and surveyed the contents. They could both use a snack. "How about some cake to go with that?"

"Sounds good." Ben sounded preoccupied, and she glanced sharply at him. He put the lid on the coffeepot and brought it to the table. Then he pulled out a chair, turned it around and straddled it, looking up at her as she poured cream into the pitcher, a slight frown on his face.

"Look, Caitlin—" he began hesitantly, then stopped to take his mug of coffee. "About what happened out there—"

"What happened out there?" Caitlin broke in hotly, meeting his eyes with feigned surprise.

"Well, I didn't mean to, well, grab you like that." A slight smile tugged at his lips. "I wouldn't want you to think—"

"Think what? That you made a habit of that sort of thing? Forget it, Ben."

"I didn't mean to—"

Oh, God, he was going to apologize! Was he going to tell her that he hadn't meant to kiss her, after all? That he was sorry it had happened, that he was—he was living with another woman and he shouldn't have done it?

"Ben! I said to forget it. We'll both forget it. As far as I'm concerned, it never happened. Okay? That's it." She took a quick gulp of her coffee and gasped as the hot liquid scorched her throat. He looked at her sharply, and she reached for the cream pitcher, as much to occupy her hands as to cool the coffee.

Caitlin had always thought the kitchen was a cheerful room, bright with a sunny yellow-and-white wallpaper, gleaming pots and pans displayed in the old dresser and sprightly white muslin curtains at the window, appliquéd with large red poppies Caitlin had cut out of a remnant of upholstery fabric. But right now the usually pleasant room hummed with awkward vibrations.

"Shall we sit in the living room?" she suggested, and Ben nodded.

"I guess you haven't been in the house since Grandma Bevan died," she said conversationally, picking up her mug and the cake plate. But Ben had already been in here, she realized with pleasure, seeing the bright fire crackling in the brick fireplace. It was comfortable and cozy, with the firelight reflected against the gleaming dark panes of glass.

Caitlin walked over to close the curtains, although against what she didn't know, there was no one but them and the van Holsts for miles around. Ben had walked to the fire and stood with his back to it, looking around the room. She watched his eyes take in the freshly painted plaster, dark woodwork and random-width wood floors covered with colorful woven rugs.

"No. But I like what you've done with it."

Caitlin smiled shyly. She was proud of the work she'd done fixing up the old house, and it was a pleasure to see that someone had noticed it.

"Here. Sit down." Caitlin handed him a piece of cake on an old Limoges plate, then curled up in a big overstuffed chair, her feet tucked under her. She took a bite, thickly slathered with cream. "Mmm."

Ben hesitated, then sat down in a chair beside the fire, opposite her. He ate the cake, put the plate beside him, then leaned back, hands clasped behind his head, long legs stretched out.

He regarded her intently for a long moment. "I'm curious about you, Caitlin Forrest."

"Mmm?" She looked up at him, just finishing her last bite. She licked her lips, an unconsciously seductive gesture that was not lost on Ben. He studied her in silence for a few seconds.

"You're very domestic, you know. Something you once said I was." His features softened slightly as he regarded her. He had her full attention now. "Don't you ever feel like sharing your talents?"

"What do you mean?"

"I wonder sometimes why you're really here, on your own like this? I know you're ambitious, you're talented, you're young, you're beautiful, you're a hard worker—too hard, I think sometimes." He laughed shortly, then went on. "I wonder sometimes why you're not married to some nice guy, settled down with a couple of children somewhere, sharing your—" he waved around the room "—many talents?"

"Maybe I've never met the right man." She answered him immediately but honestly. "And, besides, what's so unusual about it? Lots of women these days are doing things they want to do, independent things, instead of desperately chasing some man around. You live alone. Why shouldn't a single woman?'' Caitlin suddenly colored. Ben didn't live alone, not if the rumors about Jennifer Brownlee were true.

"No reason.'' He was quiet, looking into the fire. "But oddly enough, despite your obvious enthusiasm for farming—or whatever you call what you're doing here—I get the feeling that you aren't really that kind of woman.'' And he looked at her searchingly.

Caitlin turned away. He had hit a little too close to home. She wasn't really. Sometimes she longed to share her life, to be close to someone, to love and be loved. But she'd long ago decided that if it happened, it happened. She certainly wasn't going to spend her time worrying about looking for Mr. Right.

Caitlin wasn't sure she liked the turn in the conversation. She got up and went into the kitchen with the plates, returning with the coffeepot.

"More?'' she offered.

"Yes, please.'' Ben looked up at her as she bent over him, pouring. "I'm right, aren't I, Caitlin?''

His voice was low, and she knew he wanted to catch her eye. But she didn't dare look at him. She poured a cup for herself.

"So,'' she said brightly, settling herself again and ignoring his question. "How is it you happened to come by just in time for the blessed event? You didn't say.''

Ben regarded her silently for a moment, appraisingly. The message was clear: none of your business.

"I was concerned about you being alone here,'' he finally said. Then he smiled slowly, and Caitlin felt her heart jump a little sideways.

"We can get some nasty storms blowing down from the mountain and I wanted to see if I could help out with anything—you know, tie something down, whatever might be needed." He grinned. "As it turned out, I wasn't too helpful."

"But you thought I'd be out tonight."

"Hmm. Yes." He hesitated, studying her, then went on. "But I thought I'd check anyway. Just in case. Then I saw the lights in the barn."

Somehow she liked that idea, that Ben would come around, just in case she was home and needed help. He was looking out for her. Normally that would annoy Caitlin, but tonight, with the roar of the wind and the crackle of the fire and the deep silence of the mountain all around them, it seemed right.

"Well." Ben got up. "Thanks for the cake and coffee. I should go."

Caitlin got his jacket from the hook by the kitchen stove. It was almost dry.

"Thanks for coming by," she said, handing it to him. "I expect Jennifer will be wondering what's happened to you by now." Caitlin didn't know why she'd said that. Did it sound as normal, as just plain neighborly as she hoped—belatedly—it had?

"Jennifer?" Ben looked genuinely puzzled. He shrugged on the jacket.

"Yes. I heard she moved in with you last week. You needn't worry—" she paused, then got out the thought that had been rankling in her heart "—I won't mention your little, uh, indiscretion."

Ben studied her for a moment longer, eyes narrowed, then took a step toward her and seized her shoulders in his hands.

"You can't be serious. Who told you that? Gossip, that's what it is!" His eyes were blazing. "Jennifer is in her own house—in Sardis. I wasn't even here! She simply stayed at my place for a few days while hers was being painted.'' His voice was dark with anger. "Satisfied? Not—" and his voice chilled her to the bone ''—as you so rightly said once, that it's any of your business.''

Caitlin was overcome with disgust with herself, disgust that she'd ever listened to what she knew very well was gossip, disgust that she'd confronted him with her suspicions. He was absolutely right, it was none of her business. She closed her eyes briefly. He had a right to be furious with her.

She opened her eyes. Ben was still staring fiercely down at her, his strong fingers gripping her shoulders. She didn't like the look of the light that was gradually dawning in his angry eyes.

"So that's what you thought," he said, his eyes narrowed, his words slowing as though something had just occurred to him. "Back there, in the kitchen? That I wanted to apologize to you for kissing you, because of Jennifer? My 'indiscretion' as you so primly put it?'' He shook her shoulders slightly as she nodded. "That I was maybe feeling a little guilty for kissing you?'' His fingers tightened then loosened as she nodded again, miserable, and his hands slid down her arms, and he pulled her to him in an iron grip.

"Well, you're wrong, Caitlin," he growled, his voice sending shivers down her spine. "I was apologizing because things just got away from me out there.'' His eyes probed hers, refused to let her go. "No, I hadn't planned to kiss you. I thought it might have been out of line," he said softly, dangerously, then paused, his eyes darkening and filling with the same intense light that she'd glimpsed in the lightning flash on the veranda.

"But I sure as hell wanted to. Don't you know that? Lord, if you only knew how I've wanted to take you and—"

He seized her mouth with his and branded her with a hot, hungry kiss that shot instantly to Caitlin's soul and went on forever. She was so shocked at Ben's angry words and actions that for a moment she just stood there, stiff in his embrace. Then, as the heat and urgency of his body flowed into her, through his hands, through the scorching heat of his lips, through the strength of his heartbeat that she could feel hammering against hers, Caitlin felt herself melt against him. Unaware of what she was doing, her hands slowly slid up his chest until she could reach up to him, cling to him, mold her body to his, draw him even closer. Her mouth opened under his assault and he moaned in response, searching hungrily for the scent and taste of her.

Caitlin tried to pull back, then, her senses swimming. But Ben only held her closer, kissing her throat and face eagerly, growling his satisfaction at her tremulous gasp. What was happening?

Caitlin vainly tried to pull back from him again, shaking her head. But he held her against him, one hand entwined in the thick hair at her neck, the other at the small of her back, holding her close. He claimed her mouth again, this time almost reverently, his fierce strength tempered with tenderness, and Caitlin made a low instinctive sound of pleasure. This man had touched her somewhere, brought something deeply buried within her to flaming life. And she would never be the same again.

Then, as though sensing her surrender, Ben slowly kissed her lips, her cheeks, finally her closed eyelids, withdrawing from her gradually. She opened her eyes and gazed deeply into his turbulent gray ones, reveling in the light of desire she saw there still, banked now, firmly under control. She was completely and utterly shaken.

"There," Ben said huskily, holding her at arm's length, eyes lingering on her passion-glazed eyes and flushed face.

"That's what I've wanted to do for a very long time. This time, no apologies."

And with that he turned and was gone, a chilling gust of wind and rain sucked briefly into the kitchen, the only sign that he'd been there. Caitlin stood, grateful for the coolness on her hot cheeks, one hand on her heart.

He was gone.

Caitlin pulled over to the PetroCanada station at Abbotsford and rolled down the window of the van.

"Fill it, please, unleaded." She smiled at the young attendant, then reached over to the passenger seat to pull a tissue out of the box she had resting there. She blew her nose vigorously.

What a drag it was having a summer cold. She couldn't remember when she'd been sick last, and now this. In the back of the van were a dozen crates of yogurt and herb cheeses. The yogurt was for a natural food store, a new customer, and the cheeses were for a delicatessen on Granville Island. The owner had finally agreed to take her cheese on a trial basis. If she could break into the upscale shops in Vancouver's trendy Granville market, she'd have it made.

Caitlin paid for the gas and drove back onto the freeway. This cold sure didn't help. She'd woken up exhausted the morning after Ben's visit. She'd attributed her fatigue to the overwrought state of her nerves when she'd fallen into bed the night before, and dragged herself out to the barn. But by the next morning, Lucas was worried.

"Look, here, missy. Yer workin' too dang hard, that's all. Sure, get sick and do ya think them cows are gonna milk themselves?" Lucas had stomped around the barn when she hadn't answered except for a couple of loud sneezes. Lucas was right, she was working too hard. She hadn't taken a day off since she'd arrived in the spring, ages ago it seemed. But how could she? Too much depended on her.

Lucas's wife, Miep, didn't think so. When Caitlin had arrived that evening at their spotless farmhouse kitchen, to ask Lucas if he'd take over for her the next evening while she made a Vancouver delivery, the elderly Dutch woman had raised her head and regarded her keenly through her bifocals.

"Sure, sure, Caitje." Miep always used a Dutch diminutive of Caitlin's name, Little Caitlin. "And he'll take over for you the next day, too. I don't want to hear any of your excuses." She flapped her apron at Caitlin and poured her out a cup of tea, pushing it over, well laced with plenty of milk and sugar. Caitlin never took sugar in her tea. "And take a couple of these." She thrust a tin of speculaas, a crisp spice cookie, at her. Miep thought Caitlin didn't eat enough. And she considered it her sacred duty to rectify the situation.

"Lucas tells me you're sneezing already." She gave Caitlin an accusing look, daring her to deny it. Caitlin nodded and sipped the hot sweet tea gratefully.

So here she was, with three days ahead of her, all her chores at Hollyhock Farm taken over by the large and generous van Holst family. How lucky she was to have neighbors like that, she thought. Then she thought of her other neighbor and she quickly blew her nose again.

Ben. Her powerful response to Ben on Saturday night had shaken her badly. She had never dreamed, ever, of the unexpected fire that might exist under that cool, calm exterior. He had seemed a man totally in control of himself at all times. So often, Caitlin had seen him deliberately withdraw from her, keeping his distance. He was always well within the bounds of politeness, but he'd almost seemed indifferent to her. And then to—to kiss her like that . . .

She'd been caught up completely. Had Ben felt it, too? Nothing in her experience had ever come close to what she'd felt in his arms. Caitlin shivered at the memory.

Then she sighed and shifted down for the approach to the Port Mann bridge. One thing was sure, it wouldn't hurt to get away from Hollyhock Farm for a few days. She needed time to get some perspective on her feelings.

By the time Caitlin reached her friend's Kitsilano apartment, she was really feeling rotten. The bustle of the Granville Island market had made her head spin, and she was grateful for the cool and quiet of the apartment. And the way she was feeling, she was even thankful Francie wasn't in. Francie was Caitlin's old college roommate, and she'd told Caitlin to make herself at home, because she was meeting her fiancé—hadn't she told Caitlin about Tony?— for dinner. She'd be back about nine and couldn't wait to hear all Caitlin's news.

Caitlin made herself a Denver sandwich, musing over the stove as the egg congealed. So Francie had finally met a man she wanted to marry. Hmm. They'd both spent many hours giggling over each other's dates in the past. Not lately, because Caitlin had been in her own apartment for two years before she moved to Ryder Mountain. And Caitlin hadn't met anybody she was even remotely interested in marrying in all that time.

She carried her sandwich to the counter and laced it liberally with hot sauce. Maybe it would help to clear her head. Then she perched on a stool at Francie's tiny kitchen nook and took a big bite. Men had drifted in and out of her life with depressing regularity.

She'd never been short of dates, men had always found her attractive, but somehow, no one had ever really held her attention. No one had had that certain indefinable something, that magic that she knew she'd immediately recognize in the man she would want to marry. Was she an incurable romantic? Maybe.

Caitlin yawned and slumped down on the living room sofa. And that's where Francie and Tony found her when they came in two hours later. She was stretched out sound asleep, the television picture flickering in the corner. Caitlin hadn't even turned the sound up.

"Hey! This is a great way to greet an old buddy!" Francie, redheaded, a little plump and very, very happy, had flicked off the set and given Caitlin a big hug.

"Francie! Not too close, I've got some awful bug." Caitlin blew her nose again. Francie studied her with a critical eye.

"You do look rather ghastly, Caitie. Sure it's all summer cold?" She laughed as Caitlin glared at her.

"What else would it be?"

"Come here. I want you to meet Tony. Tony Benucci. Caitlin Forrest."

Caitlin nodded and smiled. Tony was a serious-looking man, thirtyish, with dark-rimmed spectacles and thinning hair.

"So," Caitlin said, looking from one to the other. "Congratulations, you two. When's the big day?"

"We're thinking about October, maybe early November." Francie gave Tony a tiny secret smile and Caitlin could have sworn she blushed a little. "We don't want to wait too long."

Tony grinned and shrugged, hands in pockets. "Well, darling?" He looked expectantly at Francie. "I'll be on my way. I expect you two have plenty to talk about." He kissed Francie, then left, with a wave to Caitlin.

Caitlin felt a pang. "He seems very nice, Francie. Why haven't I heard about him before?"

"I haven't had time! I only met him a couple of weeks ago at a party at the Seasons. But it's true what they say, Caitie," she said, her blue eyes round, "when you meet the right man, you just know."

Caitlin laughed a little uncomfortably.

"Caitie! You're staying for a couple of days, aren't you? You'll never guess who's getting married on Friday? You have to come. Lyle needs an escort." Francie had barely paused. Lyle was her brother. She picked up the coffeepot and turned to Caitlin. "Marcia! Marcia Hartley. Remember?"

"Of course. How could I forget?" Marcia had been their next-door neighbor at the flat they'd shared. Marcia had not been above knocking on their door at three in the morning to borrow a cup of flour if she'd taken a notion to make scones.

Caitlin idly picked up *The Vancouver Sun* while Francie poured the coffee. "Hey!" Caitlin paused at a head-and-shoulders studio shot of an attractive blond woman. Jennifer Brownlee. She bent to read the caption, "Wade Enterprises is happy to announce the appointment . . . Jennifer Brownlee, formerly with . . . M.B.A. from Western . . . Chilliwack offices . . ." Francie was looking over her shoulder.

"Somebody you know?"

"Yeah. Well, I've met her briefly anyway. She works for the company that loaned me some money to start up the dairy."

"Wade Enterprises?" Francie whistled and pushed over the cream and sugar. "Big time."

"What do you mean, 'big time'? I'd never even heard of them before I sent them my proposal." Caitlin folded up the paper and poured cream into her coffee.

"They're big, Caitie. Trust me. Trotter, Wade Marine, Nor'west," Francie said, naming off some industrial manufacturing and exporting companies in Vancouver. She was a market analyst. "All headed by the elusive J. B. Wade, hmm. Mystery man." Francie nodded seriously, her eyes round and blue as she reached for a second cookie.

"He's my neighbor."

"What!" Francie nearly choked on her cookie. "You live next door to J. B. Wade? *The* J. B. Wade?"

"Well, I live next door to Benjamin Wade of Wade Enterprises, if that's who you mean. You make him sound like Howard Hughes," she said crossly, picking up her coffee mug. "Ben helped me fix my fence, for Pete's sake."

Francie stared at her in amazement.

"Ben?"

"Oh, Francie. Let's forget it, okay." She yawned. She should probably go to bed if she wanted to shake this cold. But she was curious, too. Just a little. "So what's the big deal about Ben Wade anyway?"

"Ben." Francie poured herself another cup of coffee. "I don't believe this. We're talking about prime mover and shaker, J. Benjamin Wade, biggest venture capitalist on the West Coast, maybe the country, successful, private to the point of downright secrecy. Nobody I know has even seen him, although I've heard he's incredibly handsome, too."

Caitlin thought suddenly of Ben's strong features, his calm gray eyes that pierced right to her soul, the strength in the lean fingers that had burned into her flesh a few nights before, and tried to be objective.

"He's reasonably handsome, yes."

"—eccentric, supposed to be an ecologist extraordinaire—"

Caitlin thought of his expression as he had bent to show her *Gentiana crinita* "—the quarry of every socialite and gossip columnist in Vancouver, and my ex-roommate, good old Caitlin Forrest, refers to him as 'Ben.'" Francie rolled her eyes at the ceiling, but she was grinning. She winked at Caitlin. "So, what's he like, huh?"

"Nice. I don't know, Francie. It doesn't really sound like the Ben Wade I know." Then she thought of the Jaguar, the expensive clothes, the ultraprivate lodge, the No Trespassing signs. And Jennifer Brownlee had been real enough. She didn't know if she liked what she was hearing. It didn't sound like the Ben Wade she knew, but she had no doubt that he was who Francie was talking about. Then she remembered his secrecy when they'd first met, how he hadn't even told her his full name. She frowned.

"So why is everybody so interested in him?"

"Because he's rich and handsome and a bachelor, you idiot! The story is that he's still nursing a broken heart over—oh, what's her name? Some big lumberman's daughter? Lillian McQueen! That's supposed to be why he's never married. Isn't that romantic?" Francie's eyes were sparkling as she gave Caitlin the details. "'Course I don't believe it, because that was ages ago and he's supposed to have been seen with plenty of women since. Lillian dumped him at the altar and ran off with another man. A guy twice as old as Wade and twice as rich to boot. At least he was twice as rich then. Old J.B. could probably buy and sell him a couple of times over now."

Caitlin blew her nose thoughtfully. Everybody loved gossip. Especially about the rich and famous. Look at Francie. Caitlin felt slightly sick as she recalled how she'd sarcastically assumed Jennifer was living with him and how he'd accused her of listening to gossip. No wonder he'd been so angry. Lillian McQueen? Caitlin felt a cold hand grip her heart.

"You mean you never heard any of that? Back then? It was in all the papers." Francie looked incredulous.

"Maybe the papers you read. Well, I've got to hit the sack, Francie. Thanks for putting me up." And she hugged her friend and headed for Francie's spare room.

J. Benjamin Wade. What sort of a guy had she managed to get a crush on? Was that what she had—a crush on her neighbor? At least this news about Ben had put to rest any silly romantic notions she might have had—just might have had in an extremely weak moment, she told herself severely—about Ben Wade. There's no way a guy like that could be even remotely interested in somebody like her, somebody who turned down a date with him to sit with a cow in labor. Besides, she owed him a lot of money and he was holding the mortgage on her farm as collateral. Arm's length, that was the only way to deal with J. B. Wade.

Caitlin punched her pillow. Must be all this talk about weddings, she thought irritably. How come everybody and his dog all of a sudden is getting married?

Exhausted, Caitlin drifted off to sleep finally, a troubled sleep that had her dreaming of men in morning suits and women in white gowns, standing at the altar, intoning over and over again, "With this ring I thee wed, with my body I thee cherish." And every time she looked at the bride to see Francie or Marcia, she saw herself. And every time she looked at the groom she saw Ben.

Chapter Six

Just after lunch, Caitlin checked with Scott's Dairy Bar, her Granville market customer, to see if extra supplies of her Fromage du Jour had been delivered by courier yet. Mr. Scott had sold out her initial supply quickly and the extra expense of the courier was well worth it, she'd decided, to keep a potential good customer.

Mr. Scott gave her a broad grin when she arrived at his stall. "Darn good service, young lady. Now, that's what I call special delivery!"

Caitlin was puzzled. "By courier, you mean? Well, I thought—"

The manager laughed. "Some courier service you folks have got out in the valley! Bringin' the cheese around in a flamin' Jag!"

"What are you talking about?"

"Just what I said. Guy in a fancy suit came around in a Jag half an hour ago, says he's got a delivery from Hollyhock Farm. Just backed up in the loading zone out there and carted in the boxes. Cool as you please.''

Good grief! Ben? It must have been Ben. How many guys did she know with Jaguars? Wait until she saw Lucas! He was supposed to have arranged for a courier.

Still, the delivery was made, it looked like the customer was pleased as punch and that probably meant a permanent spot at Granville market. Which meant she could begin paying back Wade Enterprises even sooner than she'd planned. And that, after all, is what she really wanted, she reminded herself.

When Caitlin arrived back at Ryder Mountain the next day—she'd begged off Marcia's wedding, a wedding was the last thing she wanted to attend—she felt almost like her old self. Macleary bounded around the side of the barn when he heard the van's engine, barking his welcome. The jerseys in the pasture next to the orchard raised their heads and watched her approach, dark eyes all interest, mouths rhythmically working on tufts of grass they'd pulled up.

Caitlin got out of the van and stretched. It was so blessedly peaceful here, just the happy whine of Macleary as he wound himself around her legs and the soft sigh of the wind in the trees. Willie's little Volkswagen was parked in the driveway and Caitlin stopped in at the dairy before heading for the house.

"Caitje! We didn't expect to see you back yet!''

"Homesick, I guess,'' Caitlin said with a smile. "By the way, Willie, do you know if Lucas got my message to send down some cheese by courier on Wednesday?''

"Didn't it get there?'' The older woman looked alarmed.

"It got there all right.'' Caitlin smiled to reassure her. "No problem. It's just that the buyer said someone in a fancy car brought it in, not the courier. I was—I was wondering what happened.''

"Ah, that was Mr. Wade," Willie said. "Ya." She gave the gleaming floor one more swipe with the mop and took it over to the cleaning cupboard. "Ya. Mr. Wade was here when Miep came up, and he said he'd take care of it for me. I thought he'd just call up this—what is it? a courier?—but I guess he took it in, himself. He said he was going into Vancouver anyway."

Caitlin walked up to the house, frowning. It must just be her—no one else seemed to think it odd that J. B. Wade would be delivering cases of cheese from the back seat of his Jaguar. She had to giggle at the image that came to her mind.

There were some messages for her when she got in, calls to return. One was from Larry Sanderson, a rain check on the date they'd had to cancel. She called to confirm it. A night out was probably the best medicine for the way she felt lately.

Caitlin told herself that she was glad that Ben was in Vancouver. She didn't want to see him for a while, at least not until the memory of last Saturday's embrace had faded a little, if it ever would. Now that she had a few facts at her disposal—Francie's information had finally opened her eyes—she thought she could handle herself with a little more aplomb. The thing was to stay calm and remember: Ben's world is completely different from yours, Caitlin Forrest, and never the twain shall meet. And that, my girl, is reality.

But it was one thing to make up her mind, quite another to carry it off.

The next afternoon, Caitlin bustled around the kitchen, making a batch of her Grandma Bevan's special apricot jam and experimenting with a browned Devonshire-type clotted cream that she was thinking of introducing to her line of Hollyhock Farm products.

While the pans of cream warmed slowly in the oven, Caitlin stirred a kettle of golden preserve on top of the stove. It was a hot afternoon and she had the windows open, with a fan on to carry off the steam from her jam making. So she didn't hear the knock on her door at first, until it was repeated loudly.

"Come in!" Caitlin yelled. It was probably Willie, ready to quit for the day. She couldn't leave her kettle anyway, for fear of burning her jam. Caitlin blew at a tendril of hair that had escaped from her bandanna to fall onto her damp forehead and quickly wiped the perspiration from her upper lip with a bare shoulder. She was wearing an old pair of cutoff jeans and a cotton-knit tube top. It was too hot for anything else.

Caitlin heard the screen door slam shut.

"Willie?" She looked over her shoulder. But it wasn't Willie. Ben was leaning against the dark frame of the door, casual in tan shorts and an open shirt, regarding her with a mixture of amusement and wariness. Caitlin felt her heart give a great leap that shocked her. Get a hold of yourself Caitlin Emily Forrest, she told herself firmly, and resolutely turned back to the kettle, glad to have something to distract her.

"Hello, Caitlin." His voice was warm and deep.

A shiver ran down her spine, and Caitlin swallowed. "Hello." She looked quickly at him, then back to her jam. She raised the spoon and critically eyed the yellow stream. It wasn't separating into two flakes yet, as the books stressed, so she knew it wasn't quite ready. She stirred again. "Sorry, Ben. I can't leave this just now."

"Fine, fine." He came closer and looked over her shoulder into the pot. She was intensely aware of his nearness, of his faint unique male scent, here in her kitchen, amid the scents of sugar and jam and fresh cream.

"Mmm. Smells good," he said, then stepped back to perch on a kitchen stool.

Caitlin knew his eyes were on her, and she squirmed inside, feeling his cool gray gaze like a caress on her heated skin.

"It's apricot jam. I thought I'd better make a batch before the starlings got them all."

"Hmm."

Ben seemed quite relaxed, Caitlin thought, as she stole another quick glance at him. He was looking around the kitchen, at her arrangement of pink roses in a bowl on the dresser, at the freshly washed sterile jars awaiting the preserves.

"Ben, I'd like to thank you for taking my delivery in to Granville market for me," she began stiffly. "There was no need for you to take it in yourself. I expected Lucas to send it by courier."

"I know. Willie told me." Ben shrugged, not very interested, it seemed, his gaze on Ryder Mountain rising green and gray behind her kitchen window. "But I was going in anyway. It was no trouble."

"Thank you." She looked shyly at him, and he met her glance immediately.

"You're very welcome," he said, with a slow smile that lit his calm gray eyes and did wild things with Caitlin's pulse. She looked at her jam, flaking from the spoon now.

"Could you hand me that cloth, please?" She reached to take the cloth he'd handed to her and lifted the kettle off the stove, straining with the effort.

"Here. Let me do that." She gave Ben the wooden handle and he lifted it easily to the counter. "That where you want it?"

"Thanks. Now I've got to work fast, you'll have to stand back." Caitlin took her bottom lip between her teeth in an

IT'S FUN! IT'S FREE!
AND IT COULD MAKE YOU A

MILLIONAIRE

If you've ever played scratch-off lottery tickets, you should be familiar with how our games work. On each of the first four tickets (numbered 1 to 4 in the upper right)—there are PINK METALLIC STRIPS to scratch off.

Using a coin, do just that—carefully scratch the PINK STRIPS to reveal how much each ticket could be worth if it is a winning ticket. Tickets could be worth from $5.00 to $1,000,000.00 in lifetime money.

Note, also, that each of your 4 tickets has a unique sweepstakes Lucky Number...and that's 4 chances for a **BIG WIN!**

FREE BOOKS!

At the same time you play your tickets for big cash prizes, you are invited to play ticket #5 for the chance to get one or more free book(s) from Silhouette. We give away free book(s) to introduce readers to the benefits of the *Silhouette Reader Service*™.

Accepting the free book(s) places you under no obligation to buy anything! You may keep your free book(s) and return the accompanying statement marked "cancel." But if we don't hear from you, then every month we'll deliver 6 of the newest Silhouette Romance™ novels right to your door. You'll pay just $2.25* each—and there's no charge for shipping and handling!

Of course, you may play "THE BIG WIN" without requesting any free book(s) by scratching tickets #1 through #4 only. But remember, the first shipment of one or more book(s) is FREE!

PLUS A FREE GIFT!

One more thing, when you accept the free book(s) on ticket #5 you are also entitled to play ticket #6 which is GOOD FOR A VALUABLE GIFT! Like the book(s) this gift is totally free and yours to keep as thanks for giving our Reader Service a try!

So scratch off the PINK STRIPS on all your BIG WIN tickets and send for everything today! You've got nothing to lose and everything to gain!

*Terms and prices subject to change without notice. ©1990 HARLEQUIN ENTERPRISES LIMITED Sales tax applicable in NY and Iowa

Here are your BIG WIN Game Tickets, worth from $5.00 to $1,000,000.00 each. Scratch off the PINK METALLIC STRIP on each of your sweepstakes tickets to see what you could win and mail your entry right away. (See official rules in back of book for details!)

This could be your lucky day – GOOD LUCK!

TICKET 1
Scratch PINK METALLIC STRIP to reveal potential value of this ticket if it is a winning ticket. Return all game tickets intact.

LUCKY NUMBER

1H 451623

TICKET 2
Scratch PINK METALLIC STRIP to reveal potential value of this ticket if it is a winning ticket. Return all game tickets intact.

LUCKY NUMBER

3P 453265

TICKET 3
Scratch PINK METALLIC STRIP to reveal potential value of this ticket if it is a winning ticket. Return all game tickets intact.

LUCKY NUMBER

5M 451388

TICKET 4
Scratch PINK METALLIC STRIP to reveal potential value of this ticket if it is a winning ticket. Return all game tickets intact.

LUCKY NUMBER

9S 450771

TICKET 5
FREE BOOKS
We're giving away brand new books to selected individuals. Scratch PINK METALLIC STRIP for number of free books you will receive.

AUTHORIZATION CODE

130107-742

TICKET 6
FREE GIFT
We have an outstanding added gift for you if you are accepting our free books. Scratch PINK METALLIC STRIP to reveal gift.

AUTHORIZATION CODE

130107-742

YES! Enter my Lucky Numbers in THE BIG WIN
Sweepstakes and tell me if I've won any cash prize. If PINK METALLIC STRIP is scratched off on ticket #5, I will also receive one or more FREE Silhouette Romance™ novels along with the FREE GIFT on ticket #6, as explained on the opposite page.

(U-SIL-R 07/90) 215 HAYS

NAME _____

ADDRESS _____ APT. _____

CITY _____ STATE _____ ZIP _____

Offer limited to one per household and not valid to current Silhouette Romance™ subscribers.
©1990 HARLEQUIN ENTERPRISES LIMITED

PRINTED IN U.S.A

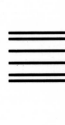

BUSINESS REPLY MAIL

FIRST CLASS MAIL   PERMIT NO. 717   BUFFALO, NY

POSTAGE WILL BE PAID BY ADDRESSEE

SILHOUETTE READER SERVICE

THE BIG WIN SWEEPSTAKES

901 FUHRMANN BLVD
PO BOX 1867
BUFFALO NY 14240-9952

NO POSTAGE
NECESSARY
IF MAILED
IN THE
UNITED STATES

unconscious gesture of concentration that Ben had seen before and began carefully pouring boiling hot preserve into her clean jars. When she'd filled a couple, she stopped to take a tin beaker from its hot-water bath on the stove and top each jar with a layer of melted paraffin. Ben took the beaker from her, and silently they completed the task, Ben topping each jar as she filled it.

"Not too thick," she instructed him, "or it will shrink from the sides of the jar when it cools. Grandma always said two thin layers are better."

"Yes, ma'am," he drawled, smiling down at her.

Caitlin laughed, then sobered. Could this really be the elusive high flyer Ben Wade that Francie had described to her, methodically topping jam jars with paraffin in her kitchen? Caitlin bit her lip to stifle a slightly hysterical giggle. How would Francie take that particular piece of information? It was too ridiculous for words!

Caitlin washed the kettle and tools she'd used for jam making, frowning slightly. Ben seemed in no hurry to say what had brought him here, but he lived only a ten-minute walk away. Dropping in unexpectedly was a normal part of country life. He obviously hadn't hurried over to apologize for his behavior on Saturday night. Did she want him to? She took a deep breath. "Ben?"

"Yes?" He was drying the canning kettle now, swiping at the enameled inside with slightly awkward gestures. He didn't look as if he were used to this sort of thing.

"Why were you here last week? Really. Willie told me you were over a couple of times?"

"I wanted to see you, Caitlin."

Ben looked at her searchingly, and she flushed under his scrutiny. She hadn't expected him to be quite so frank.

"Lucas told me you were sick, and I wanted to find out how you were," he said.

So that was it. Caitlin breathed out. He was concerned solely because he thought she'd been ill.

"Well, it was just a cold. I'm fine now," she said, somewhat peevishly. She wiped off the stove and peeked into the oven to see how her cream was doing. A light brown film was just beginning to form.

"I don't suppose it helped, getting soaked on Saturday night," he said evenly.

Caitlin's eyes flew to his; it was the first reference either had made to that night. His eyes were calm, with just that hint of wariness she'd seen when he first came in. But what had happened—really? What had been earthshaking to her, was no doubt already forgotten by him. It was just a kiss, they were both adults. She was probably exaggerating the whole thing.

"No." She paused, then went on. It didn't matter whether she was exaggerating or not. Not to her. "Ben. When I was in Vancouver I heard quite a lot of stuff about you. Stuff I didn't know."

"Oh?" He looked at her, his jaw tightened slightly. "Gossip, probably."

"Maybe. But I wondered if I could ask you a few questions, just—well, just to get things straight in my mind?" Her voice faltered slightly, but she recovered immediately, a little angry. Why did she have to ask all the questions all the time? Why didn't he ever volunteer anything?

"Sure. Fire away." Ben sat down on the stool again and regarded her seriously, a slight frown in his eyes.

"My friend Francie told me your company was very big. Is it?"

He smiled and nodded. "Quite big."

"In fact, she said that you were probably the biggest venture capital firm on the West Coast. Is that true?"

"Perhaps. Things change, but I think we're close to the top." Ben had a hint of a smile in his eyes. "What else?"

"But I thought you were just some little Chilliwack outfit!" Caitlin said, suddenly overwhelmed. Even though she'd known it, deep down, she'd wanted it not to be true.

He frowned. "What difference does it make?"

"Difference!" She stared at him. He was totally unperturbed by her questions, even seemed to welcome them. "Well, what about this mystery-man stuff? Francie says you're practically a...a recluse! That the press is always trying to track you down. Is that true?"

Ben had gotten to his feet and was walking back and forth in her kitchen, hands in his pockets. He reminded her of a big cat, energy coiled just beneath the surface. He frowned.

"I am a very private person, Caitlin." His voice was hard and he met her eyes. "I like my privacy. I prefer to be treated like an ordinary person. That's partly why I come here as much as I can. People up here on the mountain don't give a damn about the kinds of things people in the city do. I thought you knew that." His tone was faintly accusing.

"And, yes, I stay well away from the press. Why shouldn't I? I'm not a politician or a public figure to be dragged through the gossip columns like so much dead meat. Nor are the people I care about." His voice had risen slightly.

Caitlin could tell that she'd touched a nerve with her questions. She was invading his privacy, too. He didn't have to stand here and answer her questions. And yet he was.

He went on, a faint bitter twist to his firm mouth. "In my experience, the press tends to get it all wrong. And what they do get right isn't any of their damn business anyway."

"Is that why you didn't tell me who you were, at first? When you said you were just—well, just Ben?"

His eyes softened and he came to stand in front of her, tenderly tucking back the stray tendril of hair that had sprung forward again. He put his hands on her shoulders and pulled her toward him.

Caitlin tried to meet his eyes squarely, but it was hard.

"Is that what's worrying you?" he said, his voice soft, almost musing, his eyes warm with an unexpected intimacy. "I guess you're right, Caitlin. You didn't know who I was and I wanted you to think of me as just your neighbor, a simple ordinary person—which I am—not as J. B. Wade, society bachelor and all the garbage that goes with that." His mouth tightened with his last words.

A simple ordinary person is the last way she would have described him, Caitlin thought, swallowing hard. She moved away, bending to open the oven again.

The cream was ready, and Caitlin swung the two long pans out onto the counter. She tested it with a finger. "Hmm." She liked the slightly nutty taste, perhaps her customers would, too.

"What is it?"

"Something new. Browned Devonshire clot. Here, try some." Before she could think of what she was doing, she held out some of the thick brown cream on a finger and Ben stepped forward. His eyes met hers, held, burned as he slowly took her finger into his mouth and licked the cream off gently, sensuously.

My Lord, Caitlin thought with a sudden panic, quelling her instinctive reaction to snatch her hand back. As she looked into his darkening eyes, she felt the sudden insane need to touch him, to feel the heat of his body under her hands. She wanted to feel his lips on hers, wanted to inhale the sweet male scent of his skin, warm and smooth at the juncture of throat and chest and—

With a terrible effort, Caitlin pulled her hand away and turned from him, bending to the pan again. Carefully, with a large flat slotted utensil, she lifted the thickened cream off the pan and put it into a bowl. Ben had moved away. He stared out the window, and she felt his restlessness as though it were her own.

"Caitlin."

There was a new tone to his voice. Caitlin didn't like it. He was asserting control, taking charge again.

"Yes?" She didn't look up from her task.

"Any more questions?"

"No." She desperately wanted to ask about stupid things like Lillian McQueen and how many film stars he had gone out with and whether he preferred blondes, but impulsive as she was, no amount of curiosity could provoke those questions.

"Does that mean the air is clear between us now, Caitlin? You've forgiven me for not telling you certain things? From the beginning?"

His voice held a faint note of vulnerability that Caitlin found oddly appealing.

"I guess so, Ben. I certainly don't hold anything against you." She smiled at him with what she hoped was a brisk noncommittal smile. "I think we can remain good neighbors."

"Then let's go out tonight, let me take you to dinner." He grinned. "For a start."

His voice was full of suppressed eagerness. A date? Again? "I—I have plans for tonight, Ben." She didn't know what to add.

His jaw tightened slightly, his eyes narrowing, growing cooler. "Sanderson?"

"Yes. We're going to the dance at Cultus tonight. Sort of a rain check." Caitlin was annoyed with herself. She was practically apologizing to him, making excuses for going out with Larry. If he'd only known she'd rather go out with him, Ben, than a hundred men like Larry Sanderson. But there was no way around it—Ben Wade spelled danger to her, in more ways than one.

He studied her now, eyes calm, appraising. He could see the mix of emotions that fought for supremacy in her fine mobile features. Her confusion was as crystal clear to him as the secret patterns in the depths of a high mountain pool, and his inner self exulted in that.

"Ben..." she began hesitantly, eyes troubled. "Don't you think it's better this way?"

"Better? For whom?" His response was swift and unexpectedly harsh.

"For—for both of us. For—for me." Her innate honesty told him how things really were. "I really think we shouldn't see each other, like that—"

"Like what?"

"Oh, Ben! You know as well as I do." She frowned, annoyed that he was making it deliberately difficult for her. "As dates! You know, as a man and a woman!" She glared at him. Why was he being so obtuse about this? "I think we should just—just leave things the way they are. After all, I owe you a lot of money, for the farm, and you're—you're a high-powered businessman and I'm just..." Her voice trailed off. What did she really mean?

"It's best that we keep our—our relationship at arm's length. After all, we've really got nothing in common...." She paused, the words dying in her throat. Eyes locked with his, she heard herself say, barely above a whisper, "Do we?"

Ben stood studying her face quietly for a moment or two, not replying. It seemed an eternity to Caitlin. They weren't touching, but the small space between them had become almost palpable, heavy with things said and unsaid. Then

Ben's gaze hesitated for a few seconds on her lips before lifting to her eyes again.

"We do, Caitlin." His voice was nearly as quiet as hers had been. "And you know it as well as I do."

And with that he turned and went out the kitchen door.

Chapter Seven

Caitlin surveyed the crowd from where she stood at one side of the big wood-frame hall, shutters thrown wide from screened windows to let the evening breeze from the lake cool the dancers. Outside she could just see the shadows cast from the blue-white bug killer, its glare punctuated by ungodly zapping noises as night-flying insects met a sudden end. She had been sent to find a table while Larry went to the buffet.

"Wow!" Caitlin surveyed the plate he'd set down in front of her. He'd piled it with slabs of ham, macaroni salad, potato salad, a buttered roll, coleslaw, a piece of the Mennonite farmer's sausage that was a specialty in this part of the valley, mustard relish and an assortment of pickles. Nestled gingerly on one side of the plate, against the potato salad, was a sliver of lemon meringue pie.

"I didn't know what you liked, so I got a little of everything." Larry grinned as he slid into the seat beside her. "I got the pie so I wouldn't have to make two trips."

"Besides," he added, casting an admiring glance at Caitlin's slim figure in the white cotton dress, "you don't need to watch your waistline anyway."

They'd arrived at the lakeside community hall a few hours earlier. True to his word, Larry had introduced her to the locals—Caitlin was sure she'd never remember all the names—and she'd danced with at least a dozen partners. As the new face in the valley, as Lois Bevan's granddaughter and as the proprietor of Hollyhock Farm, she had been the subject of considerable interest.

"See, I knew you could do it." Larry winked at her, grinning broadly as she pushed her plate away at last. The lemon pie was gone. "I knew you didn't live on love alone up there on Ryder Mountain."

Caitlin made a light reply and Larry winked again and laughed. He was teasing her and she knew it. Love. What was it anyhow? How had Francie been so sure?

"Come on," Larry said, aware of the slight frown that belied her words. He took her hand firmly in his. "What you need is another polka to wear off that pie." And he led her back onto the dance floor.

The next dance was a switcher and Caitlin was handed, laughing, from partner to partner, her white dress flying, her sandaled feet barely touching the ground. She begged off the next one, pleading exhaustion, and stood to the side of the hall, one hand to her heaving chest, eyes sparkling. Then suddenly she saw a familiar outline across the room, and she caught her breath.

Ben. He was leaning nonchalantly against the door frame at the entrance to the hall, one hand in his pocket, narrowed eyes scanning the crowd. He had seen Larry Sanderson, dancing now with Willie's niece, and frowned slightly, his gaze finally coming to Caitlin.

Instantly, as though a current had sliced through the room, clearing all the noise and smoke and color away, his eyes burned into hers and held; she knew without thinking about it that he'd been looking for her. Her heart seemed to stop, then start again as she saw him watching, making no move to come toward her. Then, after what seemed an eternity, he did move, and Caitlin drew him forward with her eyes, the inner glow of her pleasure there for anyone to see. But only Ben was watching.

"Dance?" He stood before her, tall, dressed in dark gray, a soft black leather jacket hooked carelessly over his shoulder with one hand.

Caitlin nodded, her heart hammering, her throat dry. Why did this man always have such a devastating effect on her?

He dropped his jacket onto a nearby chair and held out his arms. Automatically Caitlin moved into them, never once feeling that she had any real choice in the matter. They fit together perfectly, and after a few moments—it would have to be a slow waltz, Caitlin thought distractedly—he pulled her closer, and she closed her eyes, allowing her cheek to rest against his chest. She could hear the deep thud of his heart, smell the clean male scent that was uniquely Ben. Every fiber of her being responded to the feel of his hands, one holding her close, the other enclosing hers, the occasional intimate touch of his thighs against hers as they moved smoothly to the music, the heat of his breath in her hair.

She'd danced this close to several of her partners tonight, and never once had she felt anything even close to what she was feeling now—warm, secure, and yet at the same time curiously excited, almost breathless, every nerve aware. Ben. Benjamin Wade, her neighbor—J. B. Wade, society bachelor, her creditor and holder of a mortgage on

Hollyhock Farm. She was in his arms, the one place she'd sworn she'd never be. Caitlin took a deep breath and looked up.

"What are you doing here, Ben? After our conversation this afternoon?" He looked down at her, one eyebrow raised in a familiar gesture, a slow smile on his lips. The look of intimacy, of secrets shared, of frank desire in his darkened eyes sent a flutter through her veins, and she felt her own response, unbidden, unstoppable, deep within her.

"Mmm. Just dancing. With the most beautiful woman in the room." Then he gripped her waist firmly and guided her gracefully through several heart-stopping turns, in total control. Several couples looked on admiringly. He lowered his voice to whisper into her ear, smiling, "I thought that was obvious."

"Of course, you idiot! That's not what I meant. Ben, let me go," she said, suddenly embarrassed at the attention they were attracting. He loosened his hand and she moved away from him slightly. He was still smiling.

"What I mean, Ben—and you know it—is why did you come here tonight?" She looked up at him. The band had moved into another number, still a waltz, but neither noticed.

"To see you."

"Me?"

"Yes, you, dear neighbor. It seems I can't get you to agree to go out with me, so I thought I'd come out and see you." Ben grinned down at her, daring her to accept his logic. "So—here I am."

"But I'm here with Larry." Larry! She'd forgotten all about him. "What in the world is he going to think?"

"Mmm." Ben looked around, in obedience to her question, then looked down at her again, a smile in his eyes that shot straight to Caitlin's heart. "Larry's enjoying himself

immensely. He's still dancing with Anna vander Veen. I
don't think he's missed you a bit."

"Oh!"

"That bother you?"

"Of course not. I've danced with dozens of men tonight." Somehow that didn't come out sounding right. Ben
laughed, a low rumble in his chest.

"So what's one more? Right?"

He pulled her close and she was forced to put her cheek
against his chest again. At first Caitlin resisted, then a lan-
guorous feeling crept over her and she didn't speak. He held
her for a moment after the music ended, then slowly—almost reluctantly Caitlin thought with a tiny thrill—he released her.

"Now. Come on. That wasn't so bad, was it?"

He was laughing at her. Caitlin, against her own well-
thought-out resolve, smiled back, a brilliant smile that
found an echo in the flush of her cheeks, the sparkle of her
eyes, and the light that suddenly sparked in Ben's. That's
how Larry Sanderson found them.

"Hey, looks like you two know each other already." He
shook Ben's hand heartily. "Good to see you, Wade. I've
been introducing Caitlin to some of the folks. Matter of
fact, she asked me out last Saturday, too." He grinned
broadly at Caitlin. "But her prize cow took a notion to
calve. How d'ya like that?"

Ben's sudden swift look at Caitlin and his raised eyebrow
showed his surprise. Reddening, Caitlin aimed a mental kick
at Larry's shins.

"Ever get stood up for a cow?" Larry continued. "Caitlin says it can get pretty lonely up there at your end of the
valley."

"I think I could do something about that," Ben drawled,
with a wink at Larry.

Caitlin could see Ben was enjoying this enormously. Larry seemed about to elaborate and she took his arm firmly.

"Well, nice to see you, Ben. Uh—excuse us—Larry, I think you're wanted over by the bandstand." And she marched him away, hotly aware of Ben's amused eyes on their retreating backs.

An hour later, Caitlin was ready to go home. Ben hadn't asked her to dance again and, unaccountably, she felt deflated. You silly goose, she scolded herself, don't forget who he is, you're better off staying well away from him. But it was no use. Everywhere she looked, she saw him, bending his head as he caught someone's conversation, whirling around some of the local girls—the prettiest ones, Caitlin thought—smiling down into their adoring faces. Or so it seemed to Caitlin.

"Enjoy yourself?" Larry put a hand on her shoulder to escort her though the door and to the darkened parking lot. It was much cooler now with a few scattered drops of rain.

"Yes. Thanks for bringing me, Larry," she said lightly. "It's wonderful to see people still enjoying themselves at an old-fashioned shindig like this." She heard a few shouts in the parking lot, slamming car doors and yelled farewells.

"Yeah." Larry was silent for a moment, then frowned slightly. "Must say I was a little surprised to see Wade here, though."

"Oh?"

"Yeah. He's a loner. Usually keeps pretty much to himself."

Caitlin digested this bit of information silently. They were at Larry's car now, and he handed her in, going around to open his door.

He started the car and put it into gear, turning to her once before he released the clutch. "Great guy, though. Everybody thinks the world of him up here." Then he let out the clutch. There was a thumping sound from the rear of the car.

"What the—?" Larry got out of the car and looked under it. "Well, how do you like that? A flat." He walked around the other side and let out a yelp. "Another one!"

"Trouble here?"

Caitlin recognized Ben's voice in the velvety darkness and cursed her relieved reaction. So he hadn't left with one of the women he'd danced with! It was a new moon and only a sprinkling of stars showed through the cloud cover.

"Yeah, damn! Couple of flats. Wonder how that happened?" Larry squatted next to Ben while they surveyed the damage. Caitlin stood beside them, hugging herself suddenly in the night air. "Looks like somebody's let the air out of the tires. Pranksters!"

"Too bad, Sanderson. Shall I send over a truck from Art's on my way by?" Art's Garage was the nearest mechanic.

"No, he'll be closed. I'll have to ring him up from the hall. Or maybe someone already has." Larry looked around him, where a couple of other drivers were cursing the teenaged male population in general, some of whom had obviously thought Saturday night at Cultus Lake could use a little extra excitement. He paused, brow knit. "This might take some time. Look, do you mind taking Caitlin home, Ben? It's on your way. It might be a while until I get this sorted out."

"Not at all. If the lady agrees, that is?" Ben turned to her.

She sensed rather than saw his grin. "I don't have much choice, do I?" Caitlin snapped rather ungraciously. "Sure you've got room for me in your car?" Now why had she said that?

"Oh, I think I could squeeze you in," Ben drawled, taking her elbow. "Right then. Good luck, Sanderson."

He loomed beside her, guiding her out of the parking lot to the shoulder where he'd parked. Trust him not to have his tires flattened, Caitlin thought peevishly. Of course—he'd arrived late, after the ambushed lot had filled.

They got in in silence, and the powerful engine instantly purred to life. Caitlin had never been in such a luxurious car before, and she settled down in her plush leather seat, stifling a yawn. She looked at Ben, sitting beside her, hand on the gearshift, the hard planes of his profile lit up with the flashing red signal light of the car ahead of them. He seemed preoccupied.

They turned onto the highway and Ben accelerated. Caitlin had made up her mind to wait until Ben opened the conversation, but he remained silent. Finally, several miles down the road, Caitlin could contain herself no longer.

"Ben?"

"Hmm?"

"Believe it or not, this damsel-in-distress stuff is not my style. Usually I manage to take care of myself." Her voice was relaxed, almost musing, as she leaned against the leather headrest, her head half-turned to study him in the dark. "So how come you just happen by whenever I need rescuing?"

"I do?"

"Sure." She yawned. "Fixing my fence, patching up my scrapes, feeding me . . . now you're driving me home."

"And you want to know if it's good luck or good management?" He smiled at her with the warm, slow smile that always struck a deep chord in her, in some mysterious place that seemed to belong as much to him as it did to her.

She glanced at him, startled a little at the way he'd put it. "Mmm. Yes. Something like that."

"I prefer to think it's good management." He laughed and glanced in the rearview mirror. "But I'm beginning to believe maybe it's good luck after all."

Then he looked at her, liking the way she looked, all in white, like an angel against the soft dark leather of the car. Or a bride. He frowned and shifted the Jaguar into overdrive. What was happening to him? He'd known his dreams, his needs, his aspirations perfectly all his life, since he'd discovered long ago he could count on only one person in this world—himself.

But now... now he didn't know. And he knew that this slip of a girl beside him was the cause of his confusion. This is not how he'd planned things at all. Was he going to allow himself to get involved with her? Really involved? Because somehow he knew with Caitlin Forrest there was no other way. And Ben Wade didn't know if he wanted to take that risk. But did he have a choice anymore?

He thought of how he'd seen her, floating, laughing, dancing at the hall, and how his insides had clenched at the thought of her in the arms of any other man, even for a moment, even for a country polka, ridiculous as that was. And yet he hadn't mistaken the way her eyes had lit up when she'd seen him....

She looked at him, puzzled. "Good luck! I haven't the slightest idea of what you're talking about." She yawned again and settled back on the seat, hugging herself quickly as she shivered. Morning would be here all too soon.

"Cold?" Ben reached one arm into the back seat and brought out his leather jacket. He draped it around Caitlin's shoulders, then looked at her once, quickly turning his eyes back to the road. She was dwarfed by the jacket, her eyes huge in her face, pale in the starlight and dim interior lights.

She snuggled down into the warmth of his jacket, breathing in his scent. She felt very tired all of a sudden.

"Ben?" Her voice was a faint murmur. "Why?"

"Why what?"

"Why'd you come tonight?" She was nearly asleep, leaning back on the headrest. Ben made an adjustment to the seat position so it would be more comfortable for her, then reached across and took her hand. His felt warm and firm around hers, comforting. He squeezed her hand gently.

"You know why." His voice was deep and quiet.

Yes, she thought sleepily, perhaps deep down she did know why.

That was the last thing she remembered until she woke up, cramped and a little stiff, in front of her own house. She turned her head, disoriented, to find Ben regarding her intently. How long had he been watching her? His right arm was stretched across the back of her seat, and her head was cradled in the crook of his elbow. She couldn't read his expression in the darkness.

"Oh!" she said, sitting up straighter. "I—I must have dozed off."

"Slept nearly all the way," Ben said. He opened his door and came around to let her out. "Easy now." He put one hand under her elbow to guide her up the steps. Macleary came around the corner of the house, whining eagerly and wagging his tail.

"Here, let me do that." Ben took her old-fashioned skeleton key and turned it in the keyhole. He held up her key, grinning down at her. "Great security. You can get these two for a buck at McLeod's."

"Thank you." She took the key from him and hung it inside the door, where it had hung in her grandmother's day. "Thanks for bringing me home, Ben. I—I appreciate it."

"Yes. Rather bad luck about Sanderson's tires," he said dryly.

Caitlin responded with a tired smile. "Well. Good night, Ben."

Ben looked at her intently for a few seconds, as though memorizing her features, then, just when Caitlin thought he'd lean down to kiss her good-night, he stepped back.

"Good night, Caitlin. Sweet dreams."

He went down the steps, hands in his pockets, practically whistling, she thought as she shut the door.

But her dreams had not been sweet. In fact, the next morning she felt as though she'd barely slept at all. When she'd closed her eyes, she'd seen a pair of gray eyes, warm as honey one moment, cold as flint the next. How could she put him firmly out of her life—where he belonged—when he elbowed his way into every cranny of her mind, invaded her dreams and preoccupied her waking thoughts?

Like now, she thought irritably, still sleepily shuffling about her kitchen, wearing her tatty old pink chenille bathrobe, trying to make her mind up whether just to opt for a bowl of granola or go all out and make pancakes after she'd brewed the coffee. Were those footsteps she heard on the porch?

"You again!" she said, not even caring how rude she sounded. She opened the kitchen screen door and pulled the old robe closer around her slender body. She had thought it might be Lucas, back from the barn. "What in the world are you doing here, Ben? It's not even eight o'clock!"

"Good morning to you, too, Caitlin," he said with a wry grin, taking in her rumpled attire, her sleep-flushed face. "You're looking lovely this morning and in your usual sweet temper." Then he strode past her into the kitchen. "Mmm. Is that fresh coffee I smell?"

"Sweet temper? Is it any wonder?" Caitlin grumbled, mostly to herself, and fastened her belt securely. She patted her tousled hair absently. Mornings had never been her best times. Ben, on the other hand, seemed his usual full-blooded, handsome self. Arrogant, too, she thought sourly.

She watched as he poured two mugs of coffee and brought them to the island counter, where she had already taken a stool. She refused to meet his eyes, just poured her cream and stirred thoughtfully.

"I was out for an early ramble." He sipped his coffee, meeting her eyes at last, over his mug. "Thought I'd drop in and see how Cinderella survived her night out. Just ordinary neighborly friendliness, Caitlin. That's what you want, isn't it?"

Caitlin studied the design on her mug, ignoring him, sipping her coffee thankfully. She never felt quite alive until she'd had her first cup or two. Finally she glanced up. He was looking at her intently, a very odd expression on his face, she thought. Amusement, irony and a faint softness, a tenderness, that gave his normally aloof features a certain vulnerability. It was an intriguing combination. She put her cup down.

"Why are you really here, Ben?" she asked quietly. "You know what I want—you've just said it. Neighbors, that's all. So what are you trying to prove?"

He looked at her and his eyes narrowed suddenly, taking in her set expression, so incongruous on her sleep-softened features.

"Ah. You're a hard woman to move, aren't you, Caitlin?" he began slowly, the strength of her resistance gradually becoming clear to him. "I thought you might have changed your mind about me since last night. Wasn't I the perfect gentleman?"

"Last night? What happened last night, except that thanks to Larry's bad luck you brought me home? And, yes, you were a perfect gentleman. But that doesn't account for why you were there in the first place! What I'd like to know is why you showed up at all." She met his steely glance with one just as unyielding.

"I don't think I have to account to you for my whereabouts, Caitlin," he said softly, a flash of diamond hardness in the gray depths of his eyes.

She heard the icy underlay of his voice and flushed. Of course he didn't have to account to her. She was getting carried away with her silly speculations. All he'd done was dance with her—once—and bring her home. She kept forgetting that while she had been busy embroidering everything he'd ever said or done with her, he probably had forgotten most of it.

For a moment they faced off, then Ben got up and went to the window. He rocked back on his heels, hands in pockets, and stood staring out for a few moments at the greengray flank of the mountain. When he turned, Caitlin was immediately aware of the altered tone in his voice, although his expression was shadowed.

"Look, Caitlin. Can't we get along? As neighbors, if that's what you want? I don't know why you're so afraid of me, I can't think it's because you really dislike me." He ran one hand through his hair in an impatient gesture.

Caitlin stopped herself—just—from blurting out that she didn't dislike him at all. In fact—   He sighed and Caitlin's heart melted, against her resolve. He was such an insular, self-reliant, mysterious man. But even though she didn't have a clue what drove him, she couldn't deny the existence of the deep, insistent tie she felt to him. Perhaps that, after all, was what she feared most.

"What do you really want, Caitlin? Do you want me to leave? Me stay on my side of the fence, you stay on yours?" He turned to her, waiting for her answer, his back to the window.

She couldn't see his face clearly, and she hesitated. "I'm sorry, Ben. I know you don't have to—to account to me—" She broke off, burying her face in her hands.

He made a slight gesture toward her, then stopped himself.

She went on, her voice shaky. She felt as though she were being torn into pieces. "I don't know what to think, Ben. I told you that I thought it was best if we didn't see each other. As dates. But you just go ahead and show up at the dance." Her eyes met his in appeal, huge in her pale face, dark hair tumbling to the shoulders of her pink robe. "What is it you want from me? What do you want me to do?" she cried, anguished.

Ben hesitated, then walked slowly back to the counter, resumed his seat and picked up his coffee, as though this sort of emotional exchange happened every day of his life.

Caitlin found the simple gesture oddly calming. She went to the stove and brought back the coffeepot, refilling their mugs.

"Do you know what I want, Caitlin? I'll be frank." His voice was low and his eyes burned into hers, calm, intent, and absolutely unswerving. "I've never met a woman like you before. I want to know you better. I want you to stop resisting me." He waved away the objections she'd been about to make. "Let me finish. I know there are things between us that you're not comfortable with—the money, the mortgage, what you perceive my position in life to be, whatever—but I don't give a damn about any of that. I find myself very—well, intrigued by you, Caitlin. I want you to allow me into your life a little. I want you to trust me. I want us to be—" he hesitated, a smile in his eyes "—friends."

Caitlin smiled weakly. The wildest, faintest, craziest hope had sprung up from the depths of her heart as he talked. He liked her! He wanted to be with her! What did it mean?

"Ben, I—I don't know what to say," she began. The fact was, she did trust him, always had, with an instinctive need that went beyond the reality of their differences. Now he was asking her to put that trust into words, into action. He was asking for her friendship. And she knew somehow that the request had not come easily to him.

Her answer glowed in her eyes, but she spoke slowly, haltingly. "I still don't think it's a very wise idea...."

"But you're willing to take a chance?" He lowered his eyes, as though not daring to anticipate her response.

She studied his features, schooled, calm, in such contrast to what he'd just said. "Yes," she said, so faintly he barely heard.

His eyes flew up to meet hers, his fierce pleasure banked hard. He didn't want to frighten her. This was such a tenuous victory.

"Did you say yes?"

She met his gaze, her eyes soft with the awareness of their new positions. She took a deep breath.

"Yes." She smiled.

"Then let me take you to dinner. Tonight." His eyes held hers, triumphant. His voice was low and urgent. He waited.

"I'd like that," she said, her eyes aglow.

Chapter Eight

Thus began several of the most tumultuous and happy weeks of Caitlin's life. Ben—the presence of him or the thought of him—dominated her days. Suspicion and distrust did not come naturally to Caitlin, and she was happy to put them behind her. And Hollyhock Dairy hit full production now, successful beyond even her wildest dreams.

Caitlin hired a regular milker, who came mornings and evenings to take care of the barn work. Willie took over more and more in the dairy, until Caitlin was mainly using her time to plan marketing strategy, to make sales forays into Vancouver and to experiment with new lines of cheese. As is the way with many innovations, the little cottage dairy catapulted to favor with a certain segment of the urban market—as Caitlin had so unerringly predicted it would— and was now in heavy demand. Restaurants, dairy bars, health food stores, delicatessens and trendy catering firms all wanted Hollyhock products and Caitlin did her best to see that they got them.

Her success seemed assured. As her income increased, Caitlin made the first in a series of payments to Wade Enterprises. She knew she would be able to pay back her debt even sooner than she had anticipated. Hollyhock's success was her success.

And, always, Ben was there.

On a particularly fine September day, a few weeks after the dance at Cultus Lake, Caitlin stood beside the barn, armed with a paintbrush and clad in a pair of shorts and an old shirt, her eyes screwed half-shut as she judged the effect of her efforts.

Her cow barn had been a constant reminder of the neglect the farm had once suffered, with its faded paint and sagging shutters. Now, with the weather fine and most of the summer bugs in hiding, she had decided to do something about it.

The shutters had been repaired with the help of Willie's handyman husband, and now Caitlin was painting the barn. She climbed up the ladder again.

Had Ben returned from Vancouver yet? She hadn't seen him for several days and had been surprised at how much she'd missed him. She smiled, half to herself, thinking of the time they'd spent together lately. After all, Ben did have responsibilities! As she did. And, by his own admission, he was spending far too much time these days at Ryder Mountain.

Unknown to her, Ben was watching her from the hillside, where he had been for the past half hour or so. He had arrived back at his Ryder Mountain estate that morning, checked in with his Chilliwack office, now in the capable hands of Jennifer Brownlee, and had hurried through the woods to Hollyhock Farm.

But just as he broke through the trees on the hillside, he had been astonished at the sight of the half-painted barn, red with white trim, and the ladder leaning against the side, a small figure in shorts and yellow shirt at the top.

"Caitlin!" he'd said, grinning broadly and shaking his head. Trust Caitlin to tackle painting a barn by herself. Then he'd found a grassy hummock to lean against and had lain back, watching her work, reveling in his secret passion for this elusive slip of a woman. She was whole, she was genuine, she was untouched by the cynicism that had tainted his life, and she was freedom and sunshine and fresh air to him.

One day, if he played his cards right, if he didn't push her, she would be his—Caitlin and everything else between here and the treeline. But he had to give her plenty of space. She couldn't be crowded, she couldn't be rushed. He thought of the way an expert angler played a trout—a noble adversary worth every second of intense, nerve-racking strategy.

The possibility of making a mistake, of losing her in the end didn't bear thinking about. But, God, the waiting was hard! When all he wanted to do was take her in his arms and...

Finally, impatient, he arose and walked casually down the hill, stopping at the bottom to lean against the gate, chin in hands. She still hadn't seen him. But Macleary had.

The old dog came over, tail wagging, with a quick yelp of greeting. Ben bent to scratch him behind the ears, and Macleary closed his eyes in bliss.

"Ben! When did you get back? What do you think of my barn? Do you think white was a good idea for the shutters? Oh, it's good to see you." Caitlin had stopped her headlong rush down the ladder, once, to point at the windows in question. Then she continued down.

"This morning. It looks fine. Yes, I do," Ben laughed, answering each of her questions. Then his eyes glinted in the late morning sunshine and he smiled down at her, where she stood facing him on the other side of the fence. "And I missed you, too, Caitlin. Very much."

Again, Caitlin regretted the unspoken hands-off understanding between them. Her first impulse, quickly curbed, had been to fly into his arms and throw her arms around him.

But it was unthinkable. Ben had not made the slightest move to touch her in the weeks since the dance. Sometimes she'd ached to have him hold her, touch her, kiss her. But he never had. Of course, she reminded herself, they were to be friends and friends only.

"Have you seen this?" Ben pulled a folded piece of paper from his pocket and handed it to her. Caitlin unfolded a photocopied page from a business publication.

"Yeah. The cheese exposition in Montreal," she read, quickly scanning the information. "I thought about going, but—"

She quickly looked up, a question in her eyes. Ben bent again to pat Macleary. His voice was carefully neutral. "Still want to go?"

"Well, of course, Ben! But it's impossible." She waved the piece of paper at the dairy, the barn. "I've got too much on the go here. And now the barn's half painted. This is happening the end of next week."

"I'll make you a deal," Ben said, straightening. He'd heard the hesitation in Caitlin's voice. He knew she wanted to go, badly. "I'll help you finish the barn and you come to Montreal with me."

"With you?"

"Yes." Ben studied her upturned face carefully, quickly. He could see her frowning as she considered the possibilities. "I've got some business in Montreal to take care of. We could go together, I do my business, you go to the exposition, we fly back."

He made it sound so simple. Willie could take over the
dairy for a few days and Freddie, her milker, had the barn
work under control. There really was no reason not to go.
Impulsively Caitlin made up her mind. She handed him the
paintbrush, blue eyes sparkling. "You're on."

They arrived in Montreal in midafternoon and checked
into their rooms at the Seigneury, on rue Sherbrooke. Caitlin looked around her with awe at the pink marbled columns, the deep pile carpet, the hushed tones of the desk
staff. Even the elevator bell had a low, discreet, almost
apologetic tone. This was luxury, this was elegance, this was
money. And this was a place where Ben was completely at
home.

Their rooms were on the third floor. Caitlin's was huge,
in tones of pink, cream and beige, and as soon as Ben and
the bellhop had left her, she crossed to the wide windows,
drew back the half-closed drapes, opened the French windows and leaned out, breathing in the indescribable scent of
the big city: iron, somehow, and tar and smoky braziers and
exotic fruit and garlic, and the smell of dust and diesel
fumes. The roar of the traffic below held the energy, the
excitement of humanity in motion, on the go, each with a
destiny to find and fulfill.

Caitlin closed the windows, kicked off her shoes and
padded through the deep pile of the carpet to the bathroom, a blaze of light and white and crystal. She washed her
face, suddenly weary from the flight but vibrating inside at
the same time with a nervous energy. Montreal was a city
where anything could happen.

She had just finished hanging up her clothes when there
was a tap at the door and Ben entered in response to her call.

"Everything okay?" he asked, glancing quickly around.
He seemed preoccupied and looked at his watch.

"Wonderful!"

"I've got a meeting scheduled this afternoon and it might run into dinner. What have you got in mind? Shopping? The cheese thing doesn't start until tomorrow, does it?" Ben was all business now, and Caitlin studied him dreamily as he talked, taking charge, making suggestions, filling her in on his itinerary.

He was wearing a dark charcoal-gray suit with creamy white shirt and perfectly knotted dark green silk tie. He'd obviously had a quick shower, because his hair was still slightly wet, and Caitlin had the sudden urge to reach up and touch it, to feel its damp darkness. He looked superb in his tailored business suit, just as he looked superb in his sweaters and blue jeans.

"Caitlin?" He glanced sharply at her. "Did you get that?"

"Mmm. Fine, Ben. Don't worry about me," she said, thinking to herself that this was the other Ben, the one she rarely saw. She suddenly flashed him a smile that took him slightly aback. "I can take care of myself. I'll do some shopping, whatever. I'll be fine."

And Ben had gone.

Two hours later Caitlin was happily tucking yet another package under her arm. She'd surveyed the fashion boutiques on exclusive rue Sherbrooke and was now tackling Crescent. Already she had purchased some soft suede boots and a loden-green cape, warmly lined with navy, that would be perfect for tramps through the woods at Ryder Mountain. Then she'd stopped at a lingerie shop, on impulse, and ended up with several new silk chemises and some frothy underwear. Caitlin might wear flannel shirts and jeans most of the time, but underneath she liked to feel completely feminine.

Now she stopped at Chez Ghislaine, a haute couture shop with no models in the window, just a discreet invitation to ring for admittance. Caitlin rang. She had never been in such rarified high fashion quarters and she was curious. Besides, Ben had asked her to accompany him to a business dinner he was hosting and she had accepted, thrilled that he had included her. Now she needed something to wear.

Caitlin tried on several dresses, twirling before the huge mirrors. Madame Ghislaine's assistant made murmuring sounds of admiration and encouragement and sometimes subtle criticism, and brought her several more garments.

Finally Caitlin made her decision. If Ben's friends were expecting a rough rambunctious amazon at the dinner party, the cheese maker from B.C.'s hinterland, they'd be disappointed. The dress was a classic strapless black silk jersey and Caitlin adored it. The plain lines emphasized her radiant health and brilliant coloring. Her hair seemed darker, her skin seemed creamier, her eyes seemed bluer. Would Ben like it, she mused, slowly turning one more time, trying to see it through his eyes.

She frowned slightly studying her reflection. Something eluded her, something trembled in the back of her mind, some difficulty. Was it not enough that she liked the dress, felt good in it, felt womanly, seductive even? No. She wanted to see her feelings reflected in Ben, in his eyes.

Suddenly the trembling in the back of her mind ceased, and her eyes flew from her dress to the image of her own face, pale in the mirror. You're in love with him, you silly goose, said her image. And you have been for a long time. Are you too stubborn to admit it?

No, she whispered back silently to the woman in the mirror. A wave of feeling, hot and cold, swept over her. No, I'm not too stubborn. It's true, I do love Ben. He's the man who completes me, who complements me, who fills the empty corners of my soul, the man I've been waiting for all my life....

"Excusez, madame? Est-ce que vous êtes malade...?" Caitlin felt the solicitous touch of the assistant's hand on her arm.

"Non, non, merci. Ça va bien, bien." Caitlin felt her feeling rush back in a flood of color. She wasn't ill—she was in love!

Caitlin paid for her purchases in a daze of happiness. She smiled brilliantly at the proprietress as she left, and thanked her several times.

Madame Ghislaine turned to her assistant. *"Vois-tu, Celine? Il n'y a rien comme une belle robe. Rien!"* And she beamed at this evidence of satisfaction rendered.

Caitlin was glad she wasn't planning to see Ben that evening; she needed time to mull over her discovery, to come to terms with it, to accept it as her very own secret. But as she fell asleep that night, bone weary with the fatigue of travel and emotion, she couldn't help but dream a little, and in her dreams Ben loved her as she loved him.

In the clear light of morning—it looked as though it would be another fine September day—Caitlin knew her discovery yesterday had changed her life. But, for Ben, she reminded herself carefully, nothing had changed. With a painful stab of insight, Caitlin realized that she had to hide her feelings, especially from Ben. After all, not for a moment did Caitlin delude herself that he felt the same way. He'd stated his position very clearly: he liked her, he enjoyed her company, she amused him, they had become friends. But he wasn't in love with her.

Then Caitlin discovered the note thrust under her door. "Came back too late to say good-night, have breakfast with me. Room 312, eight o'clock—B"

It was just after eight when Caitlin knocked lightly at Ben's door, next to hers. His room was much larger, a suite really, with separate sleeping quarters and a living-room-office area, set up now with a snowy linen tablecloth and place settings for two. To one side were two phones and a desk. Ben's briefcase stood open on it.

The door was ajar and she entered, closing it softly behind her.

"Good morning, Caitlin." Ben came out of the dressing room, wearing crisply tailored dark gray trousers and a white shirt. He was knotting his tie as he walked toward her, his eyes lit up with welcome.

She glanced down, suddenly shy. "Morning, Ben."

He narrowed his eyes briefly, studying her unusual discomfiture.

"This is very nice," she began, looking around. "I didn't realize you had your office set up here—your bedroom, uh, your bedroom is separate...."

Idiot! You're behaving like a schoolgirl! Her voice trailed off in her sudden confusion, and she walked over to the window, pretending a sudden interest in the view. Ben frowned and strode forward to stand in front of her.

"Are you all right? Sleep well?"

"Fine, Ben. " She absently reached to straighten his tie slightly, then stopped, horrified at the intimacy implicit in such a gesture. Her widened eyes flew up to meet his, puzzled, amused lights in their gray depths. He patted his tie.

"Thanks. Here, sit down." He waved her to a chair, then went to open the door. A uniformed waiter wheeled in a trolley laden with covered silver dishes. They were silent while the table was set up.

This was going to be harder than she'd realized, Caitlin thought, taking a chair and a deep breath at the same time. Dissembling was totally foreign to her naturally honest, impulsive nature. But it had to be done, she resolved; soon she'd be home again and could wind down her relationship with Ben. It was far too dangerous now for her.

"So. What time do you go to the exposition?"

"It opens at ten. I thought I'd get there a little early to meet some of the exhibitors."

Carefully, as casually as possible, Caitlin discussed her plans for the day with Ben, heard his.

"I rather like this, Caitlin," Ben said almost wistfully as he looked up from pouring the coffee. "Having breakfast with you, that is. We've never done it before."

Caitlin laughed, a little self-consciously. He was teasing her. "Done what?"

"A lot of things, having breakfast together among them." He watched her put marmalade on her toast for the second time and he frowned slightly, puzzled. "And I liked you adjusting my tie like that. It seemed—" He caught her eye and smiled. "I don't know—tender, somehow, domestic, orderly. A lot of things."

"Well, if you can't manage to make sure that your own tie is straight, I guess you need someone to do it for you," Caitlin said lightly. But that was ridiculous, because as J. B. Wade, Ben was always perfectly turned out, not a hair, not a crease out of place.

"I do, Caitlin. I do need someone."

This was said quietly, and Caitlin suddenly looked at her watch. She couldn't, wouldn't, get into a game of words with Ben. She had too much to lose.

"Well, thanks, Ben. I've got to run." She stood up suddenly and so did he.

"Shall I see you later, Caitlin? Let's have dinner together," he said, taking her hands in his. "I don't have anything planned for this evening, and I want to show you some of Montreal."

She looked up and nodded. She couldn't suddenly avoid Ben altogether; she would have to deal with each moment as it came.

"Seven o'clock? I'll come to your room."

She nodded again and looked down, fearful of what he might see in her eyes.

Ben frowned slightly and walked with her to the door. Then, when she'd gone, he stood for a moment, hands in pockets, brow creased. Something was bothering Caitlin, something was different. But what was it?

Caitlin went through the day in a blur of activity. The cheese exposition, with exhibitors displaying their products from all over the world, was held in the new Place des Saisons, a gleaming, skylit concourse of stainless steel and ceramic tile at the base of two tall office towers. Early in the day she went around, meeting exhibitors of some of the soft cheeses that she was particularly interested in, and in the afternoon she attended workshops where specialty cheesemaking techniques were demonstrated. Then there were films to watch, products to sample, lectures to attend.

At the end of the afternoon, Caitlin found herself at a champagne and cheese party, celebrating the accomplishments of the French house of Cocteau, a large cheesemaking firm in the south of France.

"Ah! Mlle Forrest!" Jean-Claude Cocteau, a younger scion of the family, bore down on Caitlin. She had talked to him earlier in the day, explaining Hollyhock Farm's concept to him and he'd been fascinated. "Tell me more about this, this—how do you call it?—cottage cheese dairy?"

Caitlin laughed merrily. "No, Jean-Claude, not a cottage cheese dairy! In fact we don't even make cottage cheese. Everything's modern and up-to-date and properly licensed, of course, but it's a cottage dairy in the sense that we make the cheese at home, from milk from our cows, and we use traditional recipes—no additives.''

The tall dark Frenchman leaned toward her while she earnestly explained. He was smiling down at her, his velvet dark eyes moving from her small pointed chin to her large blue eyes to her fine lips, to her thick dark hair, tidily pulled back into a neat coil.

''How very interesting, *mademoiselle*,'' he said smoothly, pressing another glass of champagne into her hand. ''I would very much like to hear more about this cottage dairy.'' He grinned. ''Will you honor me with your company this evening? Perhaps to dine?''

Dinner! Caitlin looked at her watch. It was quarter past six! She was meeting Ben at seven, and it was a ten-minute walk back to the Seigneury. She put her hand on Jean-Claude's arm.

''No, I'm sorry. I shall have to refuse. But thank you for reminding me of the time—I'll be late for my—my engagement.'' She quickly drained her glass and handed it back to him, empty. He observed her sudden animation, the sparkle in her eyes.

''Ah, I am devastated.'' He bent to brush the back of her hand with his lips in an extravagant European gesture of farewell. ''A most fortunate man he is, your lover.''

Lover! Caitlin blushed furiously. She smiled her farewell and hurried out into the late September sunshine.

But Caitlin needn't have worried. She wasn't late for her meeting with Ben, although she had to finish her last-minute preparations while he waited for her. She'd showered and dressed in a record eight minutes, applied the moisturizer that was all she ever wore on her face, a quick lashing of mascara and a pink lip gloss.

''I'm sorry to make you wait, Ben,'' she said, a little breathlessly, as she stepped out of the dressing room and stood for a moment, refastening the closing of her watch. He was standing, his back to the window, hands clasped behind him. She couldn't see his features at all. When he came forward, her heart suddenly hammered so loudly she was sure he could hear it, as she caught the expression on his face. His eyes were moving slowly over her, taking in the soft curves of her pink woolen jersey skirt and matching sweater.

She couldn't know how she looked to him, how the soft fabric molded and defined the young curves of her body, how it hinted at the living, breathing woman beneath, yet covered her as properly and decently and demurely as a schoolgirl. He reached up a hand to brush back a tendril of her hair that had fallen forward, then, as though unable to stop himself, he took her face between his hands and placed his lips briefly, warmly, on hers. Caitlin held her breath in surprise. Ben hadn't kissed her since the night of the storm.

Then he stepped back. "You look beautiful, Caitlin. As always." He helped her on with her coat and took her arm.

"Where to?" she said and he grinned down at her. He seemed suddenly full of energy, high spirits. Caitlin was infected by his ebullience. She laughed.

"Lead on, Ben."

Out on the street, in a crush of people, Ben hailed a cab that took them to the center of Old Montreal, and they got out and walked, for miles it seemed. Caitlin clung to Ben's arm, as much for support on the narrow sidewalks as for comfort, as he strode along, pointing out the local sights of the old quarter: the artists' studios, the *boîtes à chanson* where the local Québecois met for beer and nationalist folk songs, the tiny jewelers, the craft shops, the eating places tucked into ancient stone houses and in cobbled courtyards hung about with vines now reddening in the cool of autumn.

"Ben." She tugged on his arm as he watched a street artist who was quickly sketching a cartoon of them.

"Hmm?" He looked down at her, at her high color from
the exercise, at her sparkling eyes, the exact shade of alpine
gentians, he'd always thought. "Yes, Caitlin?"

"I'm starving. Let's eat before I absolutely faint."

"Eat? Oh, yes. That's what this was all about, wasn't it?"
Ben smiled and gave the artist some bills. The drawing
showed them with enormous heads and tiny bodies, their
features and clothing exaggerated, looking into each other's eyes, a swarm of hearts and cupids and dizzy-looking
birds around their heads. They looked at it, then at each
other and laughed.

Ben pulled her into the tiny entrance of Le Pot au Feu, a
rustic eatery specializing in Quebec food, and they shared a
plate of the house pâté, coarsely ground and rich with aro-
matic herbs. Then she sampled the tourtière, a tasty Quebec meat pie, and Ben had a thick country stew. A litre of
the local cider, crisp and dry, splashed liberally into thick
glasses completed their meal.

"You choose," Ben said, inviting her to select a dessert
for him when she'd refused one for herself, and she chose a
delicate mousse made with maple syrup and fresh cream.

"Mmm. Excellent choice," Ben said, tasting it. He put
some on a spoon and held it out to her. "Here, try some."

Caitlin took the cool confection on her tongue, savoring
the flavors of the sugar maples and the rich farmlands to the
south. She nodded and then her eyes slid away, remembering a similar offering she'd once made to him.

Ben was silent while he finished his dessert, and Caitlin
watched him, leaning forward on her elbows, chin in hands.
Her eyes were dreamy, her cheeks were flushed with the
contentment of a good meal in the company of the man she
loved.

Somehow, knowing that she loved Ben made a difference, gave a sharper edge, a poignancy to the pleasure she'd always felt in his company. She laughed harder at his small jokes, the brief touch of his fingers as he handed her her glass seemed less accidental, the low whitewashed beams of the little restaurant, the burnished copper, the very sounds of other diners, distant and detached, seemed remote, as though she and Ben were wrapped in their own cocoon of the senses, of silent wooing, of shared feelings of exquisite response. And, somehow, she knew that Ben was aware of the change that had taken place in her. No, she'd never tell him the way she felt, but she couldn't hide it, either, not from the one person who knew her almost as well as she knew herself.

"Ready to go?" Ben said, interrupting her reverie. His voice held a different note, almost of impatience. As she stood by the door, waiting for him to pay the bill a few minutes later, she studied him and felt the sudden pain of her altered position.

Oh, if only he was not who he was! If only he worked for the dairy co-op, or had Larry Sanderson's business, or was the ag rep—anybody but J. B. Wade, the man in whose debt she stood. Perhaps then she could dare to hope. But . . .

Ben took her arm and opened the door. She took a deep breath. The air was crisp and cold, and even the fumes of the city could not override the scents of autumn around them. And the sky was clear, a blanket of faint stars overhead.

"Shall we walk?" Ben's voice was low as he bent toward her.

She nodded, smiling again.

"If you get tired, we'll grab a cab."

Caitlin didn't care if they ever got back, she felt she could go on forever at his side, her hand firmly held in his larger, warm one.

They walked through the streets of Old Montreal, alive now with late-night revelers, through the exotic scents and sounds of Chinatown, then through the darkened, quieter streets of office buildings and businesses closed for the day. Finally they reached rue Sherbrooke and turned toward their hotel. Ben had been silent most of the way, answering Caitlin's occasional questions in an abstracted manner.

But when they got out of the elevator and were standing at Caitlin's opened door, Ben hesitated. He seemed slightly agitated, ill at ease, as though he wanted to tell her something. Then he met her eyes, and she almost recoiled from the intensity of emotion she saw in his. He took one step toward her.

"Caitlin, I—" he began, then halted, distracted, as the elevator purred to a stop just then and two people got out, turning to go down the hall the other way. She held the door wider for him and he stepped in, closed it and leaned against it.

He looked down at her, and she felt her heart begin to dance madly inside her chest. She swallowed hard, her voice little more than a whisper as she got out, "Yes, Ben?"

He moved closer then, not answering, but put his hands on either side of her face, forcing her gaze to meet his, the blazing heat of his eyes burning into hers, demanding an answer from her, to a question that did not need to be asked. She lowered her lashes, shocked at the overwhelming feeling that surged over her: alternating waves of tenderness, of desire, of vulnerability, of a sudden brazen impulse to throw all caution to the wind.

"Caitlin—"

She looked up at him again, heard the raw emotion in his voice, the yearning. Then she lifted her hands, sliding them under his jacket, on either side of his chest, feeling the warmth of his body smooth and solid under the thin fabric of his shirt. She tipped her head back slightly to look full at him. He was tense, his muscles tight as coiled springs under her palms.

"Kiss me, Ben."

With a groan, he pulled her to him and wrapped his arms around her, murmuring her name over and over, his words muffled in her hair. "Oh, Caitlin, Caitlin. I've waited so long for you to say that. So very long." And with that he lowered his head to her eagerly upturned face and claimed her lips with the burning, blinding evidence of his long-banked passion for her.

Chapter Nine

Ben's hands pulled her body to his, stroking, smoothing her soft curves against him until she felt that she could barely draw breath in the little space between them. The flare of his hunger, his naked desire, had shocked her and at the same time excited her beyond belief. She held him close, her mouth moving against his, tasting the faint saltiness of his lips, the smooth sweetness of his mouth, feeling the sharp nip of his teeth as he seized her lower lip. She gasped at the sensation and felt all resistance, if she had any left, melt.

"Oh, Caitlin," he growled hoarsely against her throat. Her head was thrown back, neck arched instinctively for his touch. "I've dreamed of this. You're so beautiful, so giving, so—so incredibly desirable!" He kissed her again deeply, the thrust of his tongue leaving no mistake about his need for her. She moaned against his mouth, clinging to him. She wanted to touch him, needed to feel him, skin against skin.

He groaned as he realized what she was doing, felt her slip open the buttons of his shirt and slide her palms along the hard, smooth muscles of his back.

He stiffened slightly, and Caitlin heard the swift inrush of his breath.

"Caitlin—" he whispered against her mouth, kissing her soft lips over and over again, as though he could never get enough of her, "do you know what you're doing to me?"

Her only answer was to meet his mouth eagerly. She was as hungry for him, as greedy for the taste and feel of him, as he was for her. She moved her body against his, molding herself even more closely.

Ben held her tightly and kissed her slowly, a kiss that went on forever. She felt an extraordinary languor flow through her body, each sense exquisitely tuned to Ben and to the sensations she was discovering in herself. She mused exultantly somewhere in the back of her mind: so this is what it feels like to be swept away in the arms of the man you love. All thought of restraint was gone.

She moved her hands up under his shirt to the bare skin of Ben's shoulders, loving the coiled energy, the strength, the hard planes of his back . . . and she felt him stiffen. He returned her kisses, but she could feel him slowly withdraw from her. Caitlin's brow furrowed slightly.

"What's wrong, Ben?" she whispered.

He groaned. "Wrong? Oh, Lord, Caitlin, don't you know?" He grimaced slightly. "There's nothing wrong, but if I don't stop now, I might not be able to later." He kissed her again hungrily, growling deep in his throat. "Ah, Caitlin, you are so sweet, so—I just want—"

He lifted his head and she caught her breath at the desire that burned in his gray eyes. She could do nothing, only stare wide-eyed at him, her feelings too new and too astonishingly strange to put into words.

"I want to make love to you, Caitlin, you must know that."

His eyes searched hers, and she thought she could detect a new gravity in his expression. She nodded, her eyes huge.

"But this, tonight, is too soon, too sudden. When I do, I want it to be as though it were the first time for both of us," he went on, his voice soft and caressing, like darkest velvet. "I want it to be right, Caitlin, when it happens. I want to love you so perfectly that I make you forget any other man you've ever known." His voice was fierce, his eyes blazing as he said the words to her slowly, like a vow. "I want you to be mine, Caitlin. Only mine."

His fierce need to possess her, own her, thrilled her to her core. There was no need for him to say it.

"I—I want you, too, Ben," she whispered, her heart in her eyes. Then she blushed faintly. "And there's—there's never been anyone else. I—"

"Oh, darling—" And he seized her again, kissing her cheeks, her eyes, her soft lips. Then he held her against him and she could hear the rapid thud of his heart, echoing hers for a long moment and then he began to laugh!

He was laughing! It was a reaction Caitlin had never expected in a million years! She pushed against his chest, holding herself back so she could see him. He was shaking his head, grinning down at her, an incredible tenderness in his eyes.

"What's so funny? Should I have? Been to bed with other men?" She was prepared to be angry, but Ben stopped her protestations with another quick kiss.

"No, my darling, of course not. I'm just laughing at myself." He grinned again. "At how incredibly stupid I am about you, always have been. And how you keep surprising me—over and over again. And you probably always will."

He gave her an enigmatic look. "The truth is I feel like I don't really deserve you, Caitlin. I keep expecting to wake up to find you've been a dream after all."

And he smiled and kissed her again and went out the door to return to his own room.

The memory of those moments in his arms wouldn't leave her, and she barely absorbed the lectures she attended at the cheese exposition the next day.

She realized, in the hard light of morning, how sensible Ben had been and she was grateful for that. Heaven knows, she thought with a deep surge of color, she'd never wanted anything more than to make love with him, right there, right then. That they hadn't had been solely to Ben's credit.

But now he had given her time to think it over, time to make a fully conscious, rational decision. Could matters of the heart be decided like that?

The next evening, as Caitlin got ready for the dinner Ben was hosting for his associates, she thought again about what had happened the night before. Her reflections that day had told her there could be no possible misconception about a future for her that included Ben. Now, even more urgently than before, she must sever their connection.

Perhaps she should tell him now, tonight, that she could not have an affair with him—for that's all he could possibly want.

Having an affair was contrary to her nature. She had never even been tempted before she met Ben; and she would be foolish to risk getting her own heart in any deeper, only to have it broken eventually—although perhaps it was already too late for that. Aware of a slight stab of pain, Caitlin turned to her jewelry bag. Yes, for her it was already too late.

Absorbed in her task, Caitlin combed and wound her hair into a smooth, sleek coil that she secured tightly with two enameled combs. She made up her face discreetly, then slipped on her new dress. It rustled and whispered as it settled around her and, with a wide mischievous smile on her face, Caitlin pretended to be dancing with someone and twirled several times, eyes closed. When she stopped, she whirled in astonishment as she heard the sound of someone clapping.

"Ben!" she exclaimed, the blood rushing to her face. He had come in quietly and closed the door behind him. How long had he stood there?

He walked toward her slowly, his eyes taking in every detail of her appearance. She knew she'd never looked less like a milkmaid. And he'd never looked less like her comfortable, familiar neighbor, in formal black evening wear, the stiff whiteness of his shirt lending even more authority, more power, more superb masculinity to his tall, virile figure. But he wasn't her reclusive neighbor, Ben, anymore and never would be. The time for illusions was past.

He put his hands lightly on her shoulders, and she tilted her face up to his, feeling her pulse leap instantly at the look of tenderness and desire in his eyes. He made her feel as though she were the most beautiful woman in the world, and her heart gave a great kick sideways. Was she really beautiful, desirable? She'd never, ever thought of herself that way. And yet Ben had said she was. She licked her lips; they felt dry. "You're early, Ben."

"Yes. I know. I couldn't wait any longer." And he bent down and softly kissed her, still touching her only by his hands on her bare shoulders.

Caitlin's heart felt as if it would burst at the sweetness, the tenderness. She longed to throw herself into his arms—damn the crushable dress—to kiss him, to touch, to have him touch her, as he'd done last night.

You are a fool, Caitlin Forrest, she thought, even as she reached up to kiss him, feeling his hands grip her shoulders tightly at her response, to think that you can make yourself immune to this man when you return to Ryder Mountain. This is a dangerous game that goes way, way beyond anything you've ever known before. You are playing with fire, my girl.

"Mmm. Ben," she whispered, stepping back. He followed her with his eyes, now moving slowly down her slim body.

"You look beautiful." His voice was hushed, deep. "I missed you today, Caitlin." He trailed a series of light kisses down her neck to the pulse at her throat, moving closer so that her body touched his, the lightness of the caress making it almost unbearably erotic. "I resented every meeting I had today that kept me away from you," he growled softly, and she shivered.

"Ben!" she whispered. "Don't."

"Don't what?"

"Don't do that."

"You mean this?" And he nibbled at her earlobe, then whispered, "Or this?" And he traced her lips lightly with the tip of his tongue.

Caitlin stepped back, drawing on the slim reserves of will she still had. "All of the above. Shall we go?" She looked pointedly at his watch.

"Ah, yes. We probably should. Damn." He held her jacket for her, settling it around her shoulders, then bent to brush the nape of her neck with his lips, and at her protest, said, "Just once. That's it. I promise. We've got this dinner to get out of the way and then the rest of the weekend belongs to us."

They were dining at Les Auberges. Ben's guests all arrived at about the same time, and he made the introductions, all the while never leaving Caitlin's side. She hadn't realized until now that Ben had grown up in Quebec and naturally knew French as well as English. It reminded her once again of how little she knew about him.

Caitlin was a little nervous about her role as hostess, but soon relaxed. The men, all older than Ben, gave her frank looks of admiration, and several of the women asked her about her dairy, all professing great curiosity about cows.

Caitlin hadn't yet met one couple that had just arrived. She looked up to see Ben shake the hand of a rather florid, vacuous-looking man, then turn with almost a bow, to take the hand of the woman. She was taller than her husband, exquisitely dressed, her golden cap of hair close-cropped in the latest fashion, her hand adorned with the largest square-cut emerald Caitlin had ever seen.

When she turned regally to regard the rest of the party, Caitlin saw that her eyes were green, too, the brilliant color of the gem on her finger. Her smooth brow moved a fraction as she looked at Caitlin, then she took Ben's arm and they came toward the rest of the party. The husband, Caitlin noticed, moved with alacrity to the drinks tray.

"Caitlin? Lillian Duschenes." Ben had the old look of wariness that she knew so well on his face. "Caitlin Forrest."

"How do you do?" The older woman extended her hand. "Caitlin? What a charming name! Yes, Benjamin and I are old, and—" she looked up at him, as if for confirmation "—dear friends. We go a long way back, don't we, Benjamin?"

"We knew each other once, a long time ago," Ben admitted, without the emphasis the other woman had projected.

Lillian? Caitlin felt a cold hand snatch at her heart. Was this Lillian McQueen, the woman who'd dumped Ben, according to Francie, and whom he'd never got over? Her eyes widened fractionally as she looked up at Ben.

He'd disengaged himself from Lillian's arm, under the pretext of getting her a drink, and now he handed it to her, moving away to stand with an air of quiet possession beside Caitlin. He caught Caitlin's slight look of query and instantly she read tenderness and reassurance in his eyes. She knew then, without a doubt at all in her heart, that whatever Lillian McQueen had once meant to Ben, she meant very little now. Caitlin's eyes returned his smile.

It was an interaction of a split second, but Lillian seemed to have picked up on it. "Er, Miss Forrest, are you from British Columbia, too?"

"Yes," Ben replied for her. "Caitlin is my—my neighbor."

Caitlin smiled and flushed slightly, meeting Ben's warm gray eyes. Neighbor. She didn't think the word could have been imbued with more tenderness or feeling.

Then the meal was announced and everyone moved to the table. They were in a private room and Caitlin sat at one end, opposite Ben. M. Gauthier, the grocer, sat at her right, Mme Johnston at her left. Fortunately M. Gauthier shared an interest in dairy products with Caitlin, and she soon was amusing him with information she'd picked up at the cheese exposition. Mme Johnston, a plump homemaker from Trois Pistoles, thrilled to be included in such an illustrious gathering, sat quietly, leaping into the conversation occasionally on subjects ranging from the appetites of her adolescent sons to the latest gossip about local luminaries.

"How long—I hope I am not being indiscreet, *mademoiselle*—how long have you known Monsieur Wade?" Her bright little eyes twinkled expectantly. M. Gauthier was occupied with his dinner companion on the other side.

"How long? Oh . . . since the spring."

"Not long then, really." She jabbed at a quenelle de brochet, causing it to skid slightly in its Mornay sauce. "But, perhaps long enough, too. Eh?"

What was the other woman getting at? Caitlin could see she loved gossip. "Have you known Ben for a long time then?"

"Oh, yes. For several years. Since Jean goes to l'ecole de Sherbrooke...let's see...three or four years, *oui*, since Louis has expanded into Ontario." She nodded proudly at her husband, across the table and at the other end. Louis Johnston was in computer hardware. Caitlin nodded and sipped her wine.

"Monsieur Wade was very good to Louis. Very good." Mme Johnston attacked her quenelles again, this time impaling one. She popped it into her mouth and chewed with dispatch. "Ah, they are very nice, *n'est-ce pas*?"

"I suppose you know everyone here?" Caitlin asked. The little woman lit up. She leaned toward Caitlin, inviting intimacy.

"That one, *cela* he's big with the rock stars, an impresario, *comprends*? Monsieur Wade has backed him, too, I think. His wife—poor woman, they have no children—" Whatever Mme Johnston had had to impart about the "poor woman" had to wait while the waiter replenished their glasses.

Caitlin glanced up the table to see Ben, his head inclined, listening to Lillian Duschenes. She had her slim white hand on his arm in a gesture almost of entreaty. Ben was frowning. Caitlin felt an icy ripple of fear slash through her, and an emotion she had never felt before, but knew instantly for what it was: jealousy.

"And her? Pshaw!" Mme Johnston had caught Caitlin's glance up the table, her eye sharpening as she noted the tiny signs of Caitlin's reaction. "She would like to get her claws into our Monsieur Wade, but *non*. Don't worry, he is not stupid! She had him once and she let him go. Foolish woman, eh?

"And her husband? Humph! Georges Duschenes? Somebody once, but now nobody. He's her second husband, you know? Her first one left her plenty of money, but for that kind plenty is not enough. You know Duschenes Electronics? It's on its final leg—as you say in English. I suppose that's why they are here—for the bailout. Who can say? *Ah, oui, c'est belle!*"

Mme Johnston accepted a portion of the main course, roasted partridges served with grapes and a brandied sauce. She winked at Caitlin; they were two women of the world. "Our Monsieur Wade, he is a slippery one, yes? No woman has caught him yet. He knows very well what pleases us: a little money, perhaps some jewelry, a little love. And then, poof! he is gone. But we have our memories. It is fair, eh? Love and war?" She winked again, then the good woman from Trois Pistoles thrust a fork through the breast of the partridge before her and fell to her meal with gusto.

Caitlin turned to her plate, too, shuddering slightly at the picture Mme Johnston had painted. She felt distinctly unsettled. The older woman's chatter about Ben was nothing she hadn't known or suspected, but still... And the little woman's disclosures about the course of Ben's—numerous, it seemed—affairs, made her feel slightly sick. Was she being idly sized up as next on the list? Were they all laying private odds on her chances? It seemed so...so sordid. And worst of all was the presumption by the woman beside her that she was sophisticated enough to enjoy participating in the speculation.

Had Ben's tenderness last night been a chimera after all, as she'd known full well whenever she chose to listen to hard, cold reason instead of the mad flutter of her heart?

Were his kisses nothing more than the prelude of an experienced lover to the successful launch of another affair? Just another in a very long line, according to Mme Johnston.

Why should it be any different in her case? The chase had been a little longer, perhaps, the quarry a little shyer than usual, but what was that to the jaded palate of a sophisticated man like J. B. Wade? Mere spice. Unexpected excitement. And now—she felt her flush of shame rising—he knew she was a virgin, too.

True, he'd never, ever given her any reason to think badly of him. Had he just been careful? Had she been so naive? But what, after all, could she offer him besides her body? Hollyhock Farm was all she had in the world. That, and her heart. And if she failed at her dairy—it was unlikely, but still possible—he'd have Hollyhock Farm anyway. He could foreclose. Her heart, she thought with a flash of pain, he already had.

Nonsense! she told herself. What would he want with your farm? That was ridiculous! Still, someone had wanted it once....

She shivered. Had the wine gone to her head, or had her imagination simply run away with her? This was all well beyond her depth—the knowing laughter, the nuances of cynicism, the rapierlike thrust and parry of gossip around her. She suddenly missed Macleary and the dour Lucas van Holst and the good rich smells of the earth.

Somehow Caitlin got through the rest of the evening. At the back of her mind, one thought kept plaguing her: Mme Johnston is clearly a gossip, and remember the last time you believed gossip about Ben? But the words of Mme Johnston had been too similar to Francie's disclosures for Caitlin to discount them, even if half of what she said was not true.

Somehow, she had to sever herself from Ben before it was too late. It was impossible that Ben could want anything more than an affair with her. And she would not lose her self-respect for a brief glorious moment of happiness as mistress of the man she loved.

Because ultimately—and this was hard, cold reality no matter how much she tried to avoid it—he would discard her like a too-familiar plaything, as he'd discarded so many before. Why should it be any different for her?

But it was impossible to maintain her resolution when she was finally alone with Ben in the cab. He turned to her immediately. "What's wrong, Caitlin?"

Her eyes flew to his face, disturbed that he'd known so unerringly that something was bothering her. She'd thought her performance this evening had been impeccable. "What makes you think anything is wrong?"

He reached up and pulled her chin around, tilting it up to face him. His eyes searched hers, alert, cool, penetrating. "Because I know you, Caitlin, I know you as well as I know myself. You are part of me."

She felt her heart skip a beat. How she loved him!

"Well, you don't know everything, Ben Wade, despite what you might think." She tried to move slightly away, but his arm around her was an iron band.

"Was it Lillian? Are you upset because of something you heard about me and Lillian?" He looked deep into her eyes and knew he was right when she swiftly glanced away. "I know Renee Johnston is an extremely well-primed gossip and I saw her in full flood with you." He smiled wryly.

"Lillian Duschenes? Of course not. Why should she bother me? I've only just met her."

"Ah, you silly girl." He buried his face in Caitlin's hair, inhaling its sweet scent. Then he straightened beside her, allowing her to move slightly away from him. "Well, perhaps she should bother you, Caitlin. I nearly married her once."

Caitlin's startled eyes caught his. He smiled, a dry, ironic smile. She was surprised to hear Ben refer to it so casually. "Oh."

"Is that all you're going to say?" Ben grinned again at her, this time a happy, boyish grin. "Unflappable, aren't you?"

"Well, I still can't see that it concerns me. After all, you didn't marry her, did you?" Caitlin was desperately curious to hear the story from Ben's lips, but there was no way she'd admit that to him.

"No, thank God. But it was a near thing." Ben ran his fingers through his hair in a weary gesture, a slight frown on his face as he remembered. "It was a long time ago, nine years. I was twenty-five, thought I had the world by the tail and was flattered when Lillian McQueen seemed to take an interest in me. She was Al McQueen's only daughter. You've heard of him? The lumber giant?"

She shook her head, and Ben went on. "Well, I'd done some work for him, and met Lillian. I asked her to marry me. She said yes, and I, fool that I was, was over the moon." Ben looked at Caitlin, his eyes dark with the memories. It hurt to hear Ben confess his love for someone else, even though it was so long ago.

"But I began to suspect all was not well when she put off the wedding several times. And she began avoiding me. I knew by then—a friend had thought it his duty to tell me—that she was seeing other men. But I swallowed my pride. I guess I figured that I had to stand by her. I'd asked her to marry me and I couldn't very well break it off, even though I knew by then that I really didn't want to go on with it."

He looked at her and smiled, and Caitlin's heart melted to see the tenderness in his eyes. He really did care for her. He did! How could she think otherwise?

"That shocks you, doesn't it, Caitlin? That I would have married her anyway, even knowing then that I didn't really love her?" Ben took her hand, and smiled. "Well, we do foolish things and we think foolish things and we have a great deal of foolish pride when we're young. My parents had the same kind of marriage. I thought maybe that's what marriage was—a social convenience, something you endured.

"Anyway, I'd resolved to make the best of it. Love wasn't all that important, I told myself, I'd bury myself in my work and resign myself to marrying a decorative, social butterfly of a wife, who would doubtless be a wonderful hostess but would never be the mother of my children."

Caitlin looked up at Ben. His brow was dark and his voice held an undertone of pain, almost violence. He was silent for a few moments, turning her hand over, running his thumb lightly over her palm. Then he gave her a quick, bitter smile, his lips twisted with emotion.

"Lillian saved me the trouble. She ran off with another man, Keenan McAllister. He was twice as old as her and a great deal richer than I was. That's what mattered most to her—still does. The only part that really hurt was my pride. I realized though, even at the time, what a narrow escape I'd had, and I haven't even come close to making the same mistake again." He squeezed her hand and smiled. "End of story."

They were at the Seigneury now and Ben helped her out, retaining her hand as they walked up the steps. Caitlin was silent. She didn't know what to say.

"I've never told anyone before, Caitlin, not what I told you just now. It's never mattered to me before what anyone else thought. Of course, the newspapers had a heyday with it." He flashed a quick grin down at her. "Apparently I'm still pining for Lillian McQueen, or so I hear from time to time."

She squeezed his hand, suddenly feeling a guilty twinge. She'd believed the story, too. Ben turned in the elevator so he was facing her, her hands clasped in his. He studied her face gravely, and Caitlin saw the glow of tenderness in his gray eyes. How had she ever thought them cold? "But I'm a much, much wiser man now than I was then. Shall we have coffee? In my suite?"

Caitlin drew a deep breath. The evening was not over yet. She had to make up her mind as to what she was going to do. Was she going to tell him she couldn't go on, couldn't risk having an affair with him? Now? He seemed so trusting, so unsuspecting.

He held the door to his suite for her, and she entered, moving to the center of the room to stand by the small table. What was she doing here? This is not what she'd made up her mind to do. She put one hand up to her eyes. It was all so confusing. First this sudden, earthshaking intimacy between them, when they'd been so carefully distant until this weekend. Then meeting the fabled Lillian and hearing Ben's account of their romance, and the thirdhand tidbits of gossip fed her this evening by that—that woman from Trois Pistoles. She didn't know what to think.

She looked up. Ben was ordering coffee from room service, his eyes on her. He put the receiver down.

"Caitlin?" His voice was low and puzzled. "What's wrong?" He strode toward her, his eyes taking in the uncertainty in hers. "Tell me."

It was suddenly too much for Caitlin. She needed to think. His image swam before her eyes.

"Ben, we can't go on like this—I can't," she corrected, her voice breaking, and she stumbled on, rushing to get the words out before he touched her again, before her will collapsed before the indomitability of his. "I can't—I won't have an affair with you. I couldn't stand it. I couldn't bear it if you left me when—when you got tired of me. I just want you to—to let me be. Let me alone." Her eyes, spilling over with tears, sought his. But his were implacable. "We must go back to how we were before, Ben. We must! Last night was a terrible mistake. Don't you understand?"

Something shifted in Ben's eyes, flared, and Caitlin felt a sudden panic. But then the world tilted as he pulled her to him roughly and covered her mouth with his. His kiss was fierce, angry, insistent in a way she couldn't mistake. He wanted her. And it was the same urgent, hot, elemental need that she felt flood her own veins. He held her hard against him so that she could not mistake his desire, and she melted, horrified at herself, at the mad excitement that swept through her blood even now when he obviously meant to punish her.

But then, slowly, as she clung to him, her mouth as hungry for his taste as he was for hers, his kiss changed from a harsh claim of total possession to a softer, tenderer exploration, a supplication almost. She moaned softly in her throat, utterly lost. Like a flower turning, opening to the morning sun, she could not deny Ben, could not deny the effect he had on her. Finally he released her, dragging the air back into his lungs.

"This—" he grated "—you and me—is what I understand. And so do you, Caitlin. Is this the 'terrible mistake' you're talking about?" His eyes bore down into hers, unyielding. His breathing was ragged. She shook her head, no, the tears welling afresh. With a groan he dropped his face to kiss hungrily, quickly, her cheeks, her ears, her throat. Then he wiped her tears from her cheeks with his, rough with traces of his beard.

"Caitlin." He held her close. She felt the deep, strong thud of his heart. "I need you. I need you like I've never, ever, needed any woman before. I can't let you go now that I've found you. You must believe me." He held her away from him again, searching her eyes, dark with inner pain.

Just then a knock came at the door and, with an oath, Ben released her and went to admit the attendant bringing up the coffee. Caitlin turned away while the tray was unloaded. She wiped her eyes with the back of her hand, grateful for the interruption. She listened, as though from a distance, to Ben's quiet words to the bellhop, the rustle of a bill as he tipped him, and she made up her mind.

When Ben turned, he knew, and his heart plummeted. He had not convinced her. Lord! How could he bear it? He strode past her and stood at the window, his back turned, looking out at the city for a long, silent moment. Well—? It had to be done. It was a gamble, a terrible risk, but he had no choice.

"Caitlin." He turned to her finally, his eyes full of a struggle for control that she ached to see, flicking quickly over her crumpled dress, her tear-stained face. "It's very late. I think it would be a good idea if we both thought this over."

He walked toward her, his expression as calm as he could make it, only his eyes burning. He stopped in front of her, tipped her chin up with one finger and smiled wryly down at her, a great sadness at the corners of his mouth.

"Hmm? Perhaps you'll feel differently in the morning. You might see I'm not such a beast. Hush—" He put one finger on her passion-swollen lips, where she would have interrupted to object, and went on quietly. "I don't want anything from you that you don't want to give. Freely." And he smiled lightly at her, as though he'd just told her something that had amused him in the morning paper. "I'm just an ordinary man with an extraordinary passion—you, Caitlin. Believe me."

She smiled back and nodded, but he could see the pain in her eyes. Then she left and he stared at the closed door for a very long time.

Chapter Ten

That's the family home—if you can call it that," Ben said with a trace of irony in his voice. He waved toward a huge Georgian-style stone mansion set in a grove of towering maples and oaks. In the bright light of midday, the stone looked very solid and very gray and very permanent. Caitlin looked up at Ben as he leaned casually against a sugar maple on the hillside, its red leaves dappling them with trembling shadow. She hugged her knees.

"Do your parents live here?" She knew so little about this man, only that she loved him.

Ben walked over and sat down beside her. She watched the shadows play across his handsome features: regret, pain, resignation.

"No. It's mine on paper. But my cousin took it over when I left Quebec fifteen years ago." He paused, squinting at the stone house and outbuildings below. "Dad's dead. Mother's finally free—somewhere in Bermuda, last I heard."

He looked at her, lips twisted with faint bitterness, and Caitlin felt her heart swell with pain for him.

"She does send a card from time to time, but I forget just which husband she's on now—her fifth or sixth."

"Fifth or sixth husband!" Caitlin's eyes widened. "You can't be serious."

"You sound shocked," he teased, and laughed. "Oh, Mother believes in true love, Caitlin. She just can't seem to find it." Ben plucked a stem of grass and chewed it thoughtfully, his eyes distant as he looked over the valley where he'd spent most of his childhood.

"See there? That little stone house behind the stables?" He pointed with the blade of grass, and Caitlin saw a small house built in the square Scots style of most of the small farmhouses in this area of the Eastern Townships. "That was where Jack and Madonna Doyle lived. They brought me up—mostly. Mother didn't have the time, nor the inclination. I never saw my father, except when I was sent up to town for a week before school term started."

He smiled at her, but Caitlin thought she saw the ghost of old, long-remembered pain. She remembered his vehemence when he'd said no social butterfly would ever be the mother of his child.

They'd arrived half an hour earlier, and Caitlin was still a little breathless from the long climb up the hill. At breakfast that morning, when Caitlin had come down to the dining room, she'd found Ben, freshly showered, dressed casually in tan cords and a tweed jacket, waiting for her. Apart from looking a little tired, he was the same calm, familiar Ben she'd always known. He'd put down the newspaper he was reading, waited until she'd ordered her breakfast, then proposed the trip to the townships. It was Sunday, they had planned a day of sight-seeing anyway, and he'd already arranged for a picnic hamper to be packed. Neither had mentioned the events of the previous evening.

Was it possible to dismiss so easily what had happened? Not for her, Caitlin thought as he handed her into the rented car. For him? Well, maybe she'd been right all along, a thwarted affair was no big deal in Ben's life.

And here now, listening as Ben described his solitary childhood, she thought she could see why. Ben had learned very early not to trust anyone. The hired help were the only ones he could depend on, a terrible lesson for a child to have to learn.

Ben lay back against the hill and stared up into the sky. Caitlin leaned on her elbow, looking down at him. "This place remind you of anything?" he asked, gray eyes darkening as they searched hers.

She looked around her, more to avoid his gaze than anything, absorbing the peace and quiet, the faint caress of the breeze as it lifted a lock of her hair from her cheek. Ben watched.

"Ryder Mountain?"

"Mmm. I spent a lot of time up on this hill—they call it a mountain here." He smiled, deep into her eyes, quietly sharing the joke with her, instantly apparent to anyone who'd seen the Rockies. Caitlin felt her heart turn over.

"I guess that's why I've always felt that Ryder Mountain was mine somehow, right up to the snow line." He shrugged. "I've always been a loner. By choice. And I felt that mountain was where I belonged." She nodded, her heart in her eyes. He went on, his voice so low she could barely hear it. "You love it, too, don't you, Caitlin?"

She nodded again, her eyes suddenly brimming with tears, and he reached up to brush the stray lock of hair back. She closed her eyes and a tear escaped to run down her cheek. Ben's eyes met hers, and she felt she was drowning, drowning, lost in their clear depths, and he reached up and pulled her to him.

Their lips touched, brushing gently at first. Then she held her breath as his tongue touched her lips, tracing first her bottom one, then her top. With a soft cry she opened her mouth to him, giving him access to her sweetness, longing to taste him fully, and her trembling hands went up to hold him, one on each side of his face.

How could she ever have thought she could simply make her mind up and shut this man out of her life? It was too late; he was already part of the fabric of her world. The aching sweetness of his kiss didn't satisfy her. She felt her blood flame, just as it had before. She wanted more, more— But Ben pulled back, his eyes searching hers.

"Caitlin?"

"Mmm?" She felt exhausted, torn between knowing she should not have kissed him as she had and still needing him so desperately against her, his hardness fitting intimately against her softness, his strong arms around her. She closed her eyes and lay back against the fragrant earth thick with the scent of fallen leaves and forest soil. She felt him twist and loom over her, one hand cupping the smooth curve of her cheek. She opened her eyes.

"I've thought about what happened last night." His voice was serious and very deep. "It's no good, Caitlin. I can't go back again. I need you too much. I can't pretend that I don't any longer."

She gazed up at him, her eyes wide. Pretend? What was he saying?

"Do you know why I brought you here?"

"No." She shook her head, eyes on his, then on his mouth, wanting only to reach up and draw him down to her, to make him stop talking. "Why?"

"I wanted to bring you here to ask you to marry me."

At first she thought she hadn't heard him properly. Her eyes widened, puzzled. "Marry you?" She searched his eyes for clues. Last night she'd been dithering about whether or not to risk an affair with him, and—

"Yes. I want you to marry me." His eyes burned into hers, intense with some emotion she couldn't fathom, and with something else, too—a guardedness, a vulnerability.

"Ben—I—" She blinked, struggling to sit up, but he held her down, his weight half across her body, his hands gripping her shoulders. "Ben, let me up."

"No." A half smile entered his eyes, and he bent his head to brush her lips with his again. It was unbearably erotic. She moaned softly, unable to stop herself. "Not until you say you'll marry me."

Then he took her mouth in a long, slow, drugging kiss, giving her as much as he took from her, a kiss that sent Caitlin's senses—what was left of them—reeling into the wild blue sky above, that sent her blood drumming through her veins, that had her pulling him down to her even tighter, gasping with the feeling that swept through her. Marry her? He wanted to marry her! She couldn't think, she needed to think....

"Marry me, Caitlin," he muttered hoarsely against her throat, when he finally raised his head. "I need you so much. I can't bear to let you go. You're the woman I've dreamed of, waited for all my life." He raised his head and looked down at her. "I never thought I'd find you," he whispered, and kissed her again. "I've waited long enough, Caitlin."

She felt her pulse tremble. "Don't—but don't you think this is kind of—of sudden?" It was a foolish thing to say, she knew that immediately, but she didn't know what else to say. He smiled.

"Sudden?" He laughed. "I've known you a long time, since the spring." He bent down and kissed her nose. "And sometimes I feel like I've known you forever. Why do people marry anyway, Caitlin?" He brushed his lips gently against her cheek, his breath warm in her ear. She shivered.

"Because they're in love, I suppose."

He moved his hand slightly to run his thumb along her lower lip, his eyes following the action, reading her quick shiver of pleasure. She moistened her lips with her tongue. "And would you marry me if you loved me?"

She could feel the quiet intensity in his voice.

"If—if I felt it was the right thing to do, for both of us, I suppose I would." She felt trapped by him suddenly, afraid of his eyes boring into hers, relentless. And then came the question she'd feared.

"And do you love me, Caitlin?"

Her nostrils flared slightly, her eyes widened. It wasn't fair, this inquisition! He had to let her think! Ben's grip on her, one hand at the small of her back, the other twined in her hair, tightened.

"Answer me, Caitlin!" His voice was thick with tightly controlled emotion.

She looked at him, then, at his beloved features, her gaze moving slowly over his straight nose, his square chin and jaw, his firm, sensual lips, the tiny wrinkles around his eyes. And there, deep in their clear gray depths, Caitlin saw the answer to her greatest fear.

She suddenly relaxed, realized she'd been tense with the effort of holding this one thing back from him, this one most precious thing she needed to share with him. She didn't have to be afraid. Ben knew—perhaps he'd always known—but he had to hear it from her first. His fear, she knew now, since he'd shown her his lonely childhood home, was even greater than hers. She took a deep, slow, shaky breath.

"Yes, Ben. I love you," she said, barely above a whisper, and she saw him close his eyes with the great joy of it. When he opened them, they were blazing with triumph.

"Then you'll marry me." It was no longer a question.

"Yes, I'll marry you. If you love me as I love you."

"But you know I do! I've told you that I want you, I need you, that I've waited all my life for you, just you, Caitlin Forrest, that you're part of me, that I'm part of you, that we belong together." He punctuated each phrase with a kiss, until Caitlin was practically breathless, laughing.

"Yes, but you haven't said you love me."

"Isn't that just what I've been saying?" He looked puzzled.

"No."

"All right, then." He kissed her gently on the lips, reverently. When he spoke, his voice was firm and steady. "I love you, Caitlin Emily Forrest. And I want to spend the rest of my life with you. I want to make babies with you. And I want to marry you. Right now. Today, if possible."

"Today! And how did you know my middle name?" she asked, narrowing her eyes suspiciously and blushing, slightly at his mention of babies. He wanted her—her!—to be the mother of his children.

"Because I've made it my business to know everything about you, my darling. Because I was so bowled over with you from the first week I met you that I nearly went mad sometimes thinking you'd escape from me after all. But I couldn't very well ask you to marry me right off, could I?"

"Escape? What are you talking about?" She smiled, teasing him, loving the way he looked at her, as though she truly were the only woman in the world.

"You didn't trust me, did you? You didn't trust anybody—especially anybody rich. You were so independent and so damn determined to prove yourself and stand on your own two feet. Now tell me the truth—if I'd asked you to marry me right away wouldn't you have thought something was up?''

She nodded, grinning impishly.

"I had to let you find out for yourself, in your own sweet time that you loved me. That I loved you.

"And if you hadn't discovered you loved me on your own, I would have had to try something else to convince you. Like bring you to Montreal, away from those blasted cows, and court you in earnest. You were coming around, I could tell—'' He laughed at her expression of dismay. "But I was getting impatient. Very impatient.''

He kissed her then, and again, and for a long moment they were lost in each other's arms, exploring the newness of their feelings for each other, declared finally, here in the autumn forest. At last Ben raised his head and looked down at her, his eyes glittering with emotion.

"I would have got you in the end, you know. Regardless. No matter how long it took. I couldn't allow myself to think otherwise.'' He smiled, his face alight with a happiness she'd never seen before. All his aloofness had vanished. "I never give up and I always get what I want. Remember that.''

He kissed her again lightly. "It was meant to be, Caitlin,'' he said softly, his eyes holding hers. Then he grinned and sat up, his voice firmer, "Now let's have that picnic.''

And she sat up, too, laughing, and helped him brush the leaves from her hair.

Caitlin thought she had never been as happy as she'd been that day, the day Ben asked her to marry him. And she nearly hugged herself every time she thought of the serendipity of his love for her and the future they would share.

But it was not to be.

By Tuesday—Caitlin had convinced Ben to wait until they returned to British Columbia to marry, it was impossible to be married in Montreal at such short notice anyway—the bottom of her world had started to fracture. And by Thursday the collapse was complete.

Caitlin had flown back to Vancouver late Sunday evening, despite Ben's objections. He had had to stay on in Montreal to complete some unexpected business and he'd wanted her to stay with him. Somehow—ominously, he thought later—he didn't want to let her go back to Ryder Mountain without him, without binding her to him there in Montreal, binding her irrevocably in legal marriage.

"But, Ben," she'd said, teasing him for his impatience. "We'll be married by the end of next week, in Vancouver. And I can invite a few friends, and my parents then. What are you afraid of, that I'll get away from you after all?" And she reached up to kiss him full on the mouth. He'd looked down at her, a frown creasing his brow, but his gray eyes glowing as ever with passion for her.

"If we weren't in the middle of Dorval Airport..." he'd growled, bending down to nip at her ear on the pretext of telling her something.

"You'd what?" she asked, mischievously. Ben would be the husband of her dreams. He obviously adored her, she knew he would be a marvelous lover, and they never tired of the company of each other. She sighed, tucking her arm into his to pace down the corridor with him. They were waiting for her flight to be announced. He bent down and whispered something and she blushed.

"Ah, still blushing. You vixen." He smiled down at her, patting her hand on his arm. "Still, Caitlin, I wish you'd stay, come back with me Thursday. You've nearly got away from me before, you know, several times. I couldn't bear it if anything went wrong now."

"Ben, darling." Caitlin looked up at him, her adoration for this man, her husband-to-be, shining in her eyes. "Trust me. What could possibly go wrong? And I told Freddie and Lucas I'd be back for tomorrow. Remember how you asked me to trust you once? And I did?"

He nodded and gave her a rueful look. "But you gave me some nasty moments. You may be hooked, my darling—" he grinned down at her "—but you're not landed yet. I guess I prefer to see all the ends of a deal tied up before I let go. Especially this deal."

He looked deep into her eyes and Caitlin felt her midriff tighten with a sweet, sweet ache. "I've never been in love before." Oh, how she wanted to stay here, to go back to the hotel with him and spend the rest of her life in Ben's arms. But they had to be sensible. Time enough, when they were married...

"Oh, Ben," she said, her love for him shining in her eyes, "when I think that I'd never have met you if I'd sold Grandma Bevan's farm, like everyone wanted me to."

"You were thinking of selling it?" He frowned suddenly, his eyes narrowing in surprise.

"Yes. Someone wanted to buy it—I had a couple of good offers on it—some anonymous bidder who'd approached Grandma's solicitors. Didn't I ever tell you?" She looked up at him, surprised at his continuing frown.

"No." Ben's answer was swift and surprisingly abrupt. He seemed very definite.

Caitlin looked up at him, startled. "Anyway, thank goodness I didn't take up the offer or I'd never have met you. Listen!" Her attention was caught as her flight was announced. And when she looked back at Ben, she was surprised by the odd expression on his face. He reached up to curl a strand of her hair around one finger.

"You were meant for me, Caitlin. I would have found you anywhere. Believe that." Then he bent to kiss her farewell tenderly, and her eyes filled with quick tears at the prospect of their separation, short though it was.

Caitlin watched him striding away toward the public area, tall, handsome, a slight frown on his face. God, how she loved him! Perhaps it wasn't just a dream, maybe sometimes Cinderella really did get the prince.

Lucas and Miep and Willie and Freddie and, of course, Macleary were delighted to see her back on Monday morning. She'd flown into Vancouver, spent the night with Francie, telling her of her plans to marry Ben after swearing her to secrecy; Ben wanted their wedding to be very private.

"Good grief, Caitie! Pinch me, quick." Her friend was astonished at Caitlin's news, but thrilled for her all the same. "Course, I might have known, you calling him 'Ben,' like that, right off the bat. You're a dark horse, you are. So you're beating me to the altar after all!" And Francie had wailed in mock chagrin.

"Well, well, congratulations," Lucas had said, beaming at Caitlin's obvious happiness. She'd seen no point in keeping the news from them, since the change in her circumstances might make a big difference to the dairy. "He's a deep one, that Benjamin Wade."

Caitlin's eyes had narrowed suddenly. What did he mean? Of course Caitlin had always felt Lucas had been a little suspicious where their mutual neighbor was concerned.

"Deep?"

"Well, to tell you the truth, Miss Caitlin, I never saw this comin'." He took off his cap to scratch his head. "And I do most things. Hmm. Guess there's no harm in you knowin' now you're going to marry the fellow, but Ben Wade always kinda had his eye on this place. He tried to buy it from your granny, too. We all thought he'd buy it up when she died, but then you turned up here to get it back on its feet again." He put his cap firmly back on, down to his ears. "And you've done a mighty fine job, too."

Ben? Ben had wanted this property? He'd never said so.

"Yep. Two birds with one stone, I guess you could say." Lucas heaved silently with amusement at his own joke. "Gets the girl and gets the farm thrown in. Yes, sirree. Young fella knows a good deal when he sees one, eh?" He'd winked broadly at Caitlin and she'd attempted to join in his laughter, but it was forced, and as she turned to leave the barn, her brow was clouded.

Why hadn't Ben told her he'd had his eye on the farm? Then she shrugged. It was probably just another rumor. After all, Lucas had been darn sure about Jennifer Brownlee moving in with Ben, too.

Caitlin was meeting Jennifer for lunch in Chilliwack the next day. She'd called her at Wade Enterprises to arrange another payment on her loan and to discuss the possible changes, if any, that would be made in her agreement, due to her pending marriage. She intended to pay off Wade Enterprises fully, married to J. B. Wade or not, the sooner the better. She knew Ben would probably think she was foolish, but her mind was made up. There's no way she wanted anyone to think she was marrying Ben for any reason but love.

"You're getting married?" There was a note of surprise in Jennifer's well-trained voice.

"Yes." If Jennifer wanted more information, she'd have to ask for it. She did.

"How amusing," Jennifer drawled. "No one I know, I'm sure?" Her intimation was that she and Caitlin hardly traveled in the same circles. At Caitlin's silence, she added, her curiosity getting the better of her. "Is he?"

"Actually, yes. I'm marrying Ben. Fairly soon. That's why I—"

"Ben?"

"My neighbor. Ben Wade." There was a very long pause at the other end, and when she'd recovered, Jennifer had insisted they have lunch the next day. Caitlin agreed, a little reluctantly because she felt she could barely spare the time with all she had to do over the next week or so. Nor did she look forward to the prospect of being grilled as she was sure she would be. But since she'd misread the other woman so badly once before, when she thought Jennifer had moved in with Ben, she felt the lunch would be by way of penance, to perhaps reestablish friendly relations.

"Congratulations! Or is it felicitations? I'm never sure." Late—what had she expected?—Jennifer hurried over and shook Caitlin's hand, then took a chair, looking around quickly once to see who else of any importance was lunching at the Harvest Room.

"Well, Caitlin, isn't this exciting?" Jennifer leaned toward her. "You must tell me how you managed it?"

"Managed it?" Caitlin looked puzzled.

"To catch J.B., of course! It's no secret that every well-connected woman in the province has had her eye on the elusive Benjamin Wade at one time or another." She gave Caitlin a tiny, friendly wink and smiled. "I even took a run at him myself, once, you know. But no go. Ah, well. Once burned—you must have heard about Lillian McQueen— forever shy, they say." Jennifer leaned forward, her eyes sparkling with undisguised interest.

Caitlin groaned silently. This was the sort of thing she'd hoped to avoid. Fortunately, just then the waiter arrived to take their orders. But Jennifer was not diverted.

"As a matter of fact, did you know Ben was meeting Lillian in Montreal this week? Money troubles. Poor Ben, everyone wants to borrow money from him." She leaned forward, a speculative gleam in her eye. "I believe Lillian's husband is ready to declare bankruptcy unless someone like Ben bails him out, thus her sudden interest in an old flame. Poor Lillian couldn't bear to be married to a bankrupt!"

Caitlin took a sip of her wine, hoping the slight trembling of her fingers was not noticeable to the older woman. Ben had said some business had come up unexpectedly in Montreal. He had not said that particular business involved Lillian. Would he have told her? Should he have? Perhaps he thought it was of no account.

"Mmm, yes. I met Mme Duschenes and her husband in Montreal this week, actually," Caitlin murmured, nodding to the waiter as their orders of pasta and salad arrived. "She seemed very pleasant." She hoped her seeming indifference would abort this particular line of conversation. "I'm afraid Ben's business dealings really don't concern me."

Jennifer seemed less interested then, and they discussed Hollyhock Farm arrangements with Wade Enterprises over the remainder of their meal.

"I must say, Caitlin, when I took over your portfolio, I was amazed to see you doing as well as you have been. Frankly, I would have thought your venture far too risky. But," she said, smiling, "Ben's got the right instincts, which is probably why he's the best in the business. He obviously knows a good proposition when he sees it."

Caitlin fumed silently, but then Jennifer couldn't know how sensitive she was about her own involvement with Ben's company.

"Shall we go?" Caitlin picked up her bag and put it over her arm, leaving a few bills on the table. Jennifer quickly rose and joined her.

"I do hope I haven't offended you in any way, Caitlin." Her eyes searched Caitlin's quickly and for an instant, Caitlin felt a fleeting kinship with the older woman. "After all, I've known Ben for simply ages—my brother went to school with him. I'm sure you'll be very happy together and that he's madly in love. Despite what Ben might have said about the fair sex in the past, he's not the kind of guy to marry unless he's completely smitten."

"Oh?" Caitlin felt a little confused. Now what was Jennifer hinting at? Then Jennifer dropped the final bomb in her considerable arsenal.

"Thank goodness, it's finally worked out about the property, at least. He's been after it for years." Jennifer raised her eyebrows in askance at Caitlin's startled look. "Didn't you know?" She smiled. "Oh, yes. He put in a few anonymous bids on it when the old lady died, but you wouldn't sell. Ben was furious. Told Sam Rawlings—that's the company lawyer—he'd get his hands on that farm if it was the last thing he did—even if he had to marry the granddaughter to do it. And now he is! Sam says Ben told him one woman was much like the next as long as you had money enough to keep them happy.

"Oh, Caitlin, dear, don't look like that!" Caitlin knew she was blanching despite her desperate attempt to control her shock. "Ben was only joking! He prefers the world to think he's a total cynic, even if he's not really underneath." Jennifer gave her a bright, sympathetic smile. "Funny, isn't it, how life works out sometimes?"

Absolutely hilarious, thought Caitlin, trying to focus on controlling the turbulent feelings that raged through her body. It was true! So Ben really was the anonymous bidder! Clamping down on her sudden pain, in as natural a voice as she could manage, as though idle curiosity demanded more information, she put the one question in her mind to Jennifer. "Why's he always been so keen to get his hands on Hollyhock Farm?"

"His privacy, of course, my dear! You must know Ben will do anything—anything—to protect his precious privacy. Your land is the only thing between him and crown land on that mountain. And it's not too likely that Her Majesty is going to come along and take up residence, is it?"

Jennifer had reached her car now. "Well, congratulations, anyway. I'm sure you'll both be very happy. Ciao!" She smiled brightly and waved to Caitlin, who stood leaning against the old Ford.

Somehow Caitlin managed to wave back and smile, although she felt her lips were frozen to her teeth. God! How could she have been so stupid! Sure, she'd been suspicious of Ben's motives once she'd found out who he really was...but she'd forgotten all that weeks ago, after the dance at Cultus. He'd set out to gain her trust deliberately; he'd already admitted it. And she'd fallen in love with him. She'd taken the bait: hook, line and sinker.

Love! She'd been so naive. Aha! said a nasty little voice inside her, the voice of pride, you always knew deep down the glass slipper wasn't your size.

Tears rolled down Caitlin's face all the way back to the farm. The No Trespassing signs on Ben's property, when she passed them, were scorching reminders of Ben's true motivation: to consolidate his privacy, regardless of cost. And the price had been her broken heart. She'd never, ever be able to forgive him, she stormed—never! And yet, at the same time, another voice within her begged to be heard. It can't be true! Ben would never hurt you like this—it must be a mistake!

But, no, she thought dully, as she prepared her solitary meal that evening. It all fell into place, when you thought about it, when you didn't allow yourself to be blinded by the soft, deceitful words of love. Caitlin stopped at the sink where she stood, squeezing her eyes together, a tear rolling down her cheek when she thought she'd had no more tears in her.

He had deceived her. She couldn't forgive him for that. He had deceived her right from the beginning, she realized as she started to put the pieces together. He hadn't told her his full name, he hadn't told her who he really was. True, he'd made her that loan, the only thing that got her on her feet. If he hadn't loaned her the money, she wouldn't have been able to make a go of the dairy. And then he'd have had another chance to buy the land legitimately, wouldn't he?

Caitlin's brow furrowed slightly. That part didn't make too much sense. Of course, if she'd failed, he held the mortgage on the farm and could foreclose. And, according to Jennifer, he'd had a worst-possible-scenario plan if everything else failed: he'd marry the granddaughter. She almost laughed hysterically at the irony of it. And she'd helped him out by falling in love with him!

Fact—he'd been the anonymous bidder on the farm and he hadn't told her that. Fact—even on Sunday, when she'd mentioned it, he'd had a chance to tell her the truth, and he hadn't. How much else hadn't Ben told her? How could she trust him again, even if he had explanations for all this, doubtful as it seemed? Could she marry a man she didn't trust?

Caitlin ran her hand wearily over her face. It made her brain ache to think of everything, to try to figure it out. Just when she'd finally accepted that Ben really did love her, that it was possible for him to love an ordinary person like her after all the sleek, beautiful women like Lillian and like Jennifer and like all the others that had probably been in his life, just when she'd finally dealt with her old feelings of insecurity and even jealousy—now this revelation.

Had Ben really planned to go through with their marriage as cynically as Jennifer had implied, not caring who mothered his children as long as she was reasonably young and healthy? No wonder he'd been in such a rush! Or had he hoped she'd discover his treachery, as she had, and call it off, leaving Hollyhock Farm to be sold to the highest bidder—him? Caitlin shuddered. Surely no man could be as cynical as that.

Lucas had always been reluctant to discuss Ben with her. Even he had had doubts about Ben's intentions when he'd heard of the loan from Wade Enterprises. And all Lucas's prognostications about the many ways to skin a cat!

Caitlin held her weary head in her hands. Well. She had to do something. She picked up the phone. Maybe if she talked to Ben, heard his voice, these suspicions would melt away, restore the happiness to her heart. Surely, she thought, suddenly hopeful, there would be a good reason for everything, a simple explanation. She had always trusted Ben before, instinctively.

And that's just where you went wrong, my dear, whispered the poisonous voice of pride, the one that had always insisted that she stand on her own two feet.

It was true, Ben's sweet words of love could make her believe anything. They already had. No, there was only one option left to her. To salvage anything out of this mess, she had to act first.

Chapter Eleven

The next day, Thursday, Caitlin told Ben that she'd changed her mind about marrying him. The arrival of the mailman that morning with an important-looking registered letter from the legal firm of Rawlings, Rawlings, Hudson had been the final factor in Caitlin's decision—if she'd needed one.

There it was, evidence in stark black and white of Ben's perfidy. "... Further to our correspondence with your solicitor, etc....another offer in the amount of..." Caitlin's eyes widened at the figure. It was far more than the farm was worth, even with the modernized dairy operation. Ben must have really wanted this farm. The lawyer couldn't know yet that he'd secured his interests another way! "... which our client, who prefers to remain anonymous, hopes you will find satisfactory, etc...."

Anonymous, ha! And if Jennifer hadn't let the cat out of the bag, she still wouldn't know for sure. Well, Caitlin thought, tears blurring her vision as she dropped the letter onto the kitchen table, this was all the proof she needed.

She had been dreading Ben's arrival all day, one moment her heart soaring stupidly with hope that, despite everything, all would be well and the past few days would have been just a bad dream; the next she'd plunge into despair, mourning the loss of a future with the man she loved.

Caitlin heard Ben's car arrive a little after five. Her heart fluttered wildly as she steeled herself to meet him. She wanted to fly out to the veranda the moment she heard the car door slam, to allow her emotions full rein as Macleary was doing now, yelping and dancing excitedly around Ben's feet. She saw him look once toward the house, then take the stairs two at a time.

"Caitlin!" Ben burst through the screen door, a bouquet of flowers in one hand, a quick grin of welcome on his handsome features. Caitlin stared at him across the room, her heart in her eyes, the anguish of the past days written clearly for him to see. "Caitlin," he repeated, and this time his voice was lower, puzzled concern in it and a shadow of the pain to come.

"Hello, Ben." Somehow her strangled voice got it out. This was no good. She had to tell him and she had to tell him at once. She couldn't trust her self-control to hold; she loved him too much.

"Ben, I—I've changed my mind. I can't marry you."

At the sound of her words dropping slowly into the deep silence, Ben paled visibly. His jaw tightened and with a tired gesture he tossed the flowers onto a nearby table. Then he just stood there, his expression shuttered, indescribably weary.

Say something, Caitlin whispered inside, I can't bear it like this. But Ben just stood there, his eyes raking her face.

Finally he spoke. "I see."

"Is that all you're going to say?" Caitlin cried. Didn't this just prove her suspicions, that he didn't really give a damn? "Don't you want to know why, Ben? Don't you want to know why I won't go through with this—this farce of a marriage!"

His eyes narrowed slightly at her choice of words, but he said nothing. Finally he shrugged and turned away toward the window. "I expect you'll tell me."

Caitlin couldn't believe her ears! This was not the reaction of a man disappointed in love. He sounded barely interested. "You're damn right I will! Why did you lie to me, Ben Wade? Why didn't you tell me you have always wanted to get your hands on Hollyhock Farm? That you were the secret bidder? Why—"

"I have never lied to you." The words were icy calm.

"Never lied!" She threw the lawyer's letter down onto the table beside the flowers. "What's this? Is deliberately keeping something like this from me any different?" He strode quickly to the table and scanned the letter while she continued. "First you never told me who you were. Then you kept the fact that you had anonymously bid on my land from me. Then you—"

"Damn!" Ben interrupted her tirade and threw the offer down onto the table with an angry gesture, then strode over to the window and gazed out at the north flank of Ryder Mountain, patterned with russet and gold, looking like the tawny flank of a dozing lion in the late September sun.

Caitlin stared at his back, so tall, so straight. But she could see the pain, too, in the set of his shoulders, in the agitation with which he ran his fingers quickly through his hair. He shook his head as though it were an effort to bring his thoughts back to the present. "So. What else, Caitlin?" His voice was very hard.

"What else? Jennifer told me that you'd even said you'd do anything—anything!—even marry whoever inherited the land, sight unseen, just to get your hands on Hollyhock Farm."

"Ah. So Jennifer is in on this, too, is she?" Ben's voice was low, almost mocking.

Caitlin flushed. It did suddenly sound like a litany of secondhand information. But he wasn't defending himself! If there were simple explanations, why wasn't he giving them to her?

"Ben! Don't you see why I have to call our marriage off? Aren't you going to explain it to me?" Her voice was anguished.

"No," Ben said slowly, his eyes never leaving hers. "I'm not, although you can be sure there is a very simple explanation for it all. The point is, Caitlin, you've already tried and convicted me. In absentia. You wouldn't believe me anyway, so what's the point?"

Dear God, what if there really were simple explanations for everything and she was making the biggest mistake of her life, just because her pride had been so terribly wounded? That Lucas knew, that Jennifer knew, that everyone knew but her— But, no, the offer was no figment of her fevered imagination, its very expensive bond burning a hole in the hall table beside the forgotten bouquet at this very moment.

Ben was silent, staring at her. Caitlin felt she could barely hold his level gray gaze, the pain in her own heart and the pain she felt for him almost overwhelming her.

When he finally spoke, his voice was very low. "And you believe all of this? You believe all this—of me?"

It was the only statement he'd made so far that had even a hint of appeal in it. He waited. Caitlin's heart and inner soul cried out, No, I know you'd never do this to me, Ben, never! But the tears ran down her face and she was silent.

"Well, Caitlin. I am very sorry that it has come to this. I had hoped—" His voice faltered slightly and he broke off, turning away from her. He worked to reassert the iron control that had always served him so well. Then he faced her again.

"Life is a risky business, isn't it?" His eyes burned into hers and she ached to see the flash of self-mockery in his. "Hmm? Love's a gamble, too—the biggest—and I guess I've lost. I prefer winning, naturally—" Ben smiled then, a twisted smile of pain that Caitlin felt like a knife in her heart. "But I've lost before, Caitlin. I can handle it."

He stopped for a moment, studying her. Then he lifted his hand in a slight gesture of farewell. "Well, I guess that's that. I shall..." He hesitated, cleared his throat, then went on, his voice very deep and very serious, "I meant what I said, Caitlin. I shall always love you. Good-bye." And he turned and went out the screen door.

Slam! The bang of the door galvanized Caitlin. She ran to the door and out onto the veranda.

"Ben! Isn't there—? Can't we—?" She didn't know what she wanted to say, but she was desperate to know if there was any chance at all, any explanation, any...

"No, Caitlin. I understand. I know you thought you loved me." He was looking up at her from where he stood, the car door half-opened, the sun in his eyes. Then he smiled, a bitter smile. "But it wasn't enough, was it?"

Caitlin watched him go down the driveway, then turn onto the public road. He never once looked back even though Caitlin waved foolishly, weakly, the tears streaming down her face, until long after he'd vanished from sight.

Then began such a time of black pain that Caitlin wondered how other people had survived broken hearts, how she would ever survive. She threw herself into her work at Hollyhock Farm, getting up at dawn to help Freddie in the barn, working well into the night on her books and her marketing plans in an effort to banish the ghosts of what might have been. The very success of Hollyhock Farm mocked her dreams and made her victory hollow. What was the success of her dairy, she asked herself bitterly, when she had forfeited the only thing that really mattered to her?

She had to rebuild her life without Ben, she told herself. After all, a few short months ago she'd never even heard of J. B. Wade. After all, she told herself sensibly, people were disappointed in love every day and they went on to put the pieces back together. Time heals, everyone said so. But it was no use. Caitlin was not the same person she'd been a few short weeks ago, and her friends were worried.

"How's about Willie and I take over for you this weekend, Caitje?" Lucas had offered in his gruff way, one morning in the barn. He'd noticed the gaunt shadows under Caitlin's eyes, the dullness in her eye. She'd never mentioned Ben, either, not since that first day she got back from Montreal. "Go to Vancouver, get some rest, have a little fun."

Fun? Caitlin looked up at him, her face pale. When she slept she dreamed of Ben and awoke, damp with tears of grief; when she couldn't sleep, she tossed and turned, visions of him in her head, their conversations together turning endlessly in her mind, taunting her with all she'd thrown away.

For Caitlin could see it from Ben's point of view now. After all, he had his pride, too. And how many times was he going to have to explain away hearsay and soothe Caitlin's foolish fears? How many times was he going to have to reassure her of his love? How many times was he going to have to ask her to trust him?

"What do you say?" Lucas was pressing her.

Life couldn't go on like this. It wasn't fair to her friends at Ryder Mountain. Caitlin knew she had to make up her mind. She accepted Lucas's kind offer and went to stay with Francie for a few days. She unburdened her heart to her friend—not sparing herself—and came back to the farm, full of new resolution: she had to get away from Ryder Mountain for a while and she had to get her life back into focus.

It was a crisp, chilly late October afternoon ten days later, the kind that Caitlin loved the best. The leaves still clung to the trees, but they had turned to vibrant shades of red and russet and brilliant gold. Caitlin had just come in from the orchard, where she'd been to collect some late apples, the crisp sweet windfalls that had been touched again this morning with frost. Ryder Mountain's upper reaches were dusted with a very light fall of snow, the first of the year. It made the wind, blowing down in light gusts, cold and pure and had put extra color in Caitlin's cheeks.

"Brrr! Winter's coming," she remarked conversationally to Macleary, where he'd taken up a warm position behind the big wood range. Caitlin lifted the cast-iron lid, gave the fire a poke, pushed in a few more sticks, as she'd seen her grandmother do so many times, then replaced the heavy lid. She pushed the kettle to the middle of the range. A hot cup of tea would be wonderful.

The tramp about the upper hills and the orchard had been a leave-taking of sorts. Caitlin was leaving Hollyhock Farm for a couple of weeks at least, maybe forever. Everything here reminded her of Ben, always would, and his absence had not become any less painful over the past couple of weeks. If anything, she felt the ache deeper. She needed time away to find out if she could come back and function again.

Once, just after she'd got back from the visit to Francie's, she'd wandered over to his place, half-thinking in her heart of hearts, that if she saw him, if he was there, if... But she'd been shaken to see the lodge shuttered and locked. The dogs were gone, all was secured for the winter, perhaps forever. The wind, chasing the dried leaves down the driveway, had left an indescribable feeling of melancholy in Caitlin's soul. She'd left then, vowing never to return.

Caitlin took her cup of tea into the living room and drew the blinds against the lengthening shadows outside. A bright fire burned in the hearth just as it had the night Martha had had her heifer calf, the night Ben had kissed her, and the night she'd felt their souls touch for the first time.

Was it as long ago as that? Caitlin blinked quickly, briskly. There was no point in thinking about what might have been. Martha's calf was long since weaned and part of the replacement herd.

But she felt oddly restless and more than once got up to peer out at the lengthening shadows. Lucas's daughter Willie and her husband, Jan, were set to take over the dairy for the next month. If she came back to stay, Willie was prepared to stay on at the dairy, leaving Caitlin to concentrate on marketing. If she decided not to come back—Caitlin felt her heart squeeze at the very thought.

She loved this piece of land, and the farm was part of the very fabric of the dairy. She couldn't just sell out and start another dairy somewhere else, away from Ryder Mountain. Farming was not in her blood; the cottage dairy had just been a way of proving herself and allowing her to stay on the stony thirty acres she and Lois Bevan had loved so much.

Caitlin sighed. There was so much to think about. But the time had come to make some tough decisions. She was leaving in three days, right after Francie's wedding.

Caitlin went back into the kitchen, rinsed her cup and saucer and smiled at Macleary, who looked up at her mournfully from his position near the wood stove, his tail thumping once on the worn linoleum.

"You're a good friend, Macleary," she said, with a smile at the old dog. The van Holsts would take care of him while she was gone. But what would happen to the old dog if she never came back?

She looked at the clock. Five past five. A casserole of lamb stew was ready to go into the oven, and she poked up the fire once more, throwing on a chunk of alder. Macleary sat up suddenly, ears pricked and went to the door, whining with excitement.

"Out you go," Caitlin said. As soon as she'd opened the door, he was off like a shot toward the garden. She was convinced the dog had extrasensory perception sometimes, the way he seemed to sense marauders like the raccoon that came down from the mountain to stuff his cheeks with fresh corn from time to time, or the maverick squirrel that boldly rummaged through the contents of Macleary's dish whenever the dog went indoors.

The garden looked forlorn now in the deepening dusk, with most of the harvest put up and preserved during happier days, just a few stumps of brussel sprouts and kale left in the stony soil. Someone like Francie would tot up the dollars and cents in a businesslike way, deciding rationally whether or not the hard labor was worth the harvest. But Caitlin knew she'd do it all again if she could.

She reached for the gingham apron that hung beside the sink and tied it around her waist. She'd just get a salad ready. Caitlin paused, listening. Was that a car? Who could be coming at this time?

She rinsed her hands and dried them, seeing bright headlights stab through the near-darkness and turn into her lane. Macleary let out a noisy welcoming bark. Perhaps it was Francie, Caitlin thought, pleased. She had said she might come up for a quick visit before the wedding.

There was a sharp rap at the door, and Caitlin went to open it, a slight smile of anticipation on her lips.

"Ben!" Her shock showed on her face as the color drained from it. One hand went to her breast in an unconscious gesture.

"Hello, Caitlin."

His voice was exactly as she'd remembered it: low, modulated, caressing. She felt her heart hammer and her pulse leap, and for a few seconds she felt as if she couldn't get her breath properly. Every sense was exquisitely, painfully alert. He was standing just outside the screen door under the porch light, hands jammed into the pockets of his leather jacket. Macleary sat adoringly at his feet, tail thumping, tongue lolling.

"What—what are you doing here?" It was stupid, but it was the first thing that came to her mind, suddenly stunned at the sight of him. He looked older somehow, weary, his hair longish in the back and rumpled, as though he'd run his hands through it many times on the drive up.

"I've brought you something, Caitlin."

He smiled then, a slow smile, with just a hint of irony, that sent the color flooding back into her face, her heart thumping loudly in her chest.

"May I come in?" he asked.

Brought her something? "Oh! Yes, yes, of course. For heaven's sake, come in. You must be freezing out there." She held the door open wide for him, moving back as he brushed by her, the touch, even of his clothing, sending jagged currents of awareness down her spine.

"Well! Isn't this a surprise? I thought it might be Francie—just driving up before her wedding, you know—" She knew she was babbling and stopped, swallowing hard. She wished he would stop looking at her like that, his eyes intent, his face carefully impassive. Of course—he'd probably heard via the mountain telegraph that she was thinking of selling. It had been no secret, and Lucas knew all the details.

"How—how are you, Ben?" She bent down to avoid his gaze and absently patted Macleary, who had sneaked in when she had opened the door.

"Well. And you?" He'd hesitated, and his eyes were hooded, a muscle moving faintly in his jaw. He looked down at her slim figure slowly, taking in the glossy hair, dark as a raven's wing, the faint shadows under her eyes, the blue-and-white checked apron over her long corduroy skirt, small feet clad in woolly red stockings peeking out below the apron.

"I—I'm fine." She turned away. "Come in. Sit down. Would you like some coffee?"

"Caitlin—"

At the sound of his voice, strong and urgent, she turned back, afraid of what she would see. She felt panic rise in her chest until she could barely breathe, and then, at the look in his eyes, she felt the panic slowly ebb and fade away.

"Yes?" Why was he looking at her like that? He reached into his jacket pocket and pulled out a piece of paper.

She frowned. "What's that?"

"What I've brought you, Caitlin." He unfolded it and held it out. "Your mortgage." She blanched and looked up at him, her eyes huge in her pale face, hands clenched behind her back. He hesitated, holding her gaze, then walked over to the hearth and tossed the document into the dancing flames. Then he turned back to her, his face full of pain.

"I wasn't trying to get your farm, Caitlin. Not after I met you. You took me by complete surprise the first time I saw you picking rocks in your grandmother's garden." His voice was very quiet and deep. "Once I'd met you, you were all I ever wanted." Her eyes flew to his, widened in surprise. "You still are."

"Oh, Ben..." Her voice was a whisper. Hope—infinitesimal, foolish, faint—began to flutter weakly in her breast. Tears sprang to her eyes.

"I love you, Caitlin. I always will. And I want you back again. I want us to have another chance." His voice was low and husky with emotion, but his eyes still were wary. He was afraid she'd turn him down again!

Caitlin's amazement showed in her expression, transparent to him as always: shock, pleasure, incredible hope. And then, the weeks between them vanishing in an instant, she threw herself into his arms, with a broken cry.

"Ben. Oh, Ben. I love you so." She looked up at him, tears glittering in her eyes and whispered, "Oh, what an idiot I've been." Ben's answer was to cover her mouth with his, possessing her finally with his kiss.

She'd ached for his touch for so long. His mouth was warm and delicious and demanding and incredibly exciting. He kissed her like a man who'd been half-starved, desperate for the one elixir that would make him whole again.

He needed her, with a terrible hunger, to fill the void in him he hadn't been able to fill or forget since they'd been apart.

She clung to him, molding her softness against him. Finally Ben broke from her, his breathing ragged, a suspicious moisture in his eyes.

"My darling. My darling, Caitlin. Is it really true?" He held her back, forcing her to look up at him, his eyes tired but filled again with the fierce joy she remembered. "Look at me." His voice was rough. "Don't ever leave me again." She shook her head, biting her lip to hold back the tears. "I couldn't bear it, Caitlin. I've gone through hell without you. I love you too much."

And he covered her mouth again in a sweet, slow, passionate kiss that left her limp and trembling, exulting in their hunger for each other. When he raised his head to look down into her eyes, his held the light of triumph. "Say it, Caitlin. Say you're mine."

She looked up into his face, saw the blaze of love in his eyes and responded simply, truthfully, from the depths of her being, "I'm yours, Ben. I always will be."

"Dear God!" Ben said, and bent his head to rest his forehead against her shoulder for a long moment. She felt a shudder go through him. When he raised his head, he kissed her again tenderly. "My darling, can you ever forgive me?"

"Forgive you?" she whispered. "There's nothing to forgive. I only pray that you can forgive me my lack of faith in you, Ben." Her voice broke, and a tear escaped to slide down her cheek. Ben kissed it away.

"I know, I know, darling," he said, looking deep into her eyes. "I was hurt terribly when you didn't trust me enough to believe in me without question. But I was wrong to expect blind trust from you without telling you anything at all about myself. It was so important to me that you want me for myself, not for what I represented, that I put you through hell, too. I'm sorry. My pride's to blame, I'm afraid. Even the bid on the farm.

"Sure, I'd bid on it. But that was before I'd met you, Caitlin. Unfortunately—" he grimaced "—I hadn't got around to telling Sam Rawlings to back off. He was just doing his job. He knew I wanted this farm and was prepared to do anything I had to do to get it.''

"Even marry the granddaughter?'' She grinned up impishly at him.

"Absolutely!'' He laughed and kissed her soundly again. Then he paused and studied her flushed cheeks and brilliant eyes. She looked like a woman well and truly in love. In love with him. His heart swelled with happiness, and he swept her up into his arms and carried her to the sofa before the fire, settling her on his lap, nestled against him.

"I've loved you almost from the day I met you, Caitlin. I said to myself, what kind of woman takes the time to build a fence out of stones? My kind, I decided. I'd never met anyone like you before.'' He frowned faintly. Was he remembering his mother, or Lillian?

"You see, Caitlin,'' he said, his eyes seeking hers, "most of the women I'd ever known, including my own mother, who stuck me in boarding school at the age of eight, had been motivated by money—how to get it, how to spend it, how to get more of it.'' Ben's mouth twisted with a hint of the bitterness she'd seen before when he'd mentioned his family. "You were different. I'd almost despaired of ever meeting anyone like you.

"Then, there on the very farm I was so desperate to buy, was the woman of my dreams. You hit me like a thunderbolt, Caitlin. Beautiful, intelligent, independent, ambitious and—I hoped—ready to fall in love with someone like me.''

"Oh, Ben!'' Caitlin blushed. "Don't be silly. I was just trying to get my own little dream off the ground, the dairy. It wasn't like that at all.''

"See? Modest, too. Trouble was, you were so independent, so natural, so unassuming, that you actually didn't trust anyone with a lot of money. You didn't trust me. Am I right?'' He looked down with a gleam of amusement. ''I admit that threw me. I was used to money opening doors for me, not slamming them in my face.''

''But you didn't tell me all that when we first met.''

''A good thing, too. Or you would have been put off right from the start. This way, I think you were at least a little, shall we say curious? by the time you found out.''

''More than curious,'' she said, nuzzling his neck, planting soft kisses at the base of his throat, where dark silky hairs showed above his shirt.

''Hey!'' Ben growled, and bent down to kiss the nape of her neck and the curve of her ear. ''Do you want to listen to this or not?''

''Mmm. Not really,'' Caitlin murmured, kissing him again. Then she suddenly sat bolt upright and sniffed. ''Ben! The stew! It's in the oven. Quick!'' And she'd leaped out of his arms and dashed into the kitchen.

But the casserole wasn't burned at all. It was perfect. Ben laid two places on either side of the bowl of late apples, their rosy polished cheeks reflecting light from a candle he'd found in the kitchen dresser. Sleeves rolled up, face flushed with happiness, Caitlin tossed the salad. They'd have cheesecake for dessert. What else? she thought, smiling.

''Caitlin—'' Ben came up behind her and put his arms around her, pulling her close. His voice was low in her ear, his breath ruffling her hair.

''Yes?'' She looked up at him backwards, leaning against him, a half-smile on her happy face.

''Marry me.''

She nodded, her heart in her eyes.

''Tomorrow.''

He looked very stern, and she nodded again, smiling.

"And if for some reason we can't get married in Chilliwack tomorrow, because it's Friday or some fool thing, we're going to Reno. Okay?"

And she nodded again, delighted at his low growl, his loving eyes on her.

He bent down to kiss her nose lightly, then turned her in his arms, and planted a kiss firmly on her mouth. "Because this time I'm not leaving here until we're married."

"I wouldn't let you—neighbor," she teased, the joy shining in her eyes.

*   *   *   *   *

COMING NEXT MONTH

#736 VIRGIN TERRITORY—Suzanne Carey
A Diamond Jubilee Book!
Reporter Crista O'Malley had planned to change her status as "the last virgin in
Chicago." But columnist Phil Catterini was determined to protect her virtue—
and his bachelorhood! Could the two go hand in hand...into virgin territory?

#737 INVITATION TO A WEDDING—Helen R. Myers
All-business Blair Lawrence was in a bind. Desperate for an escort to her
brother's wedding; she invited the charming man who watered her company's
plants...never expecting love to bloom.

#738 PROMISE OF MARRIAGE—Kristina Logan
After being struck by Cupid's arrow—literally—divorce attorney Barrett Fox
fell hard for beautiful Kate Marlowe. But he was a true cynic.... Could she
convince him of the power of love?

#739 THROUGH THICK AND THIN—Anne Peters
Store owner Daniel Morgan had always been in control—until spunky security
guard Lisa Hanrahan sent him head over heels. Now he needs to convince Lisa
to guard his heart—forever.

#740 CIMARRON GLORY—Pepper Adams
Book II of *Cimarron Stories*
Stubborn Glory Roberts had her heart set on lassoing the elusive Ross Forbes.
But would the rugged rancher's past keep them apart?

#741 CONNAL—Diana Palmer
Long, Tall Texans
Diana Palmer's fortieth Silhouette story is a delightful comedy of errors
that resulted from a forgotten night—and a forgotten marriage—as Long,
Tall Texan Connal Tremayne and Pepi Mathews battle over their past...and
their future.

AVAILABLE THIS MONTH

#730 BORROWED BABY
Marie Ferrarella

#731 FULL BLOOM
Karen Leabo

#732 THAT MAN NEXT DOOR
Judith Bowen

**#733 HOME FIRES BURNING
BRIGHT**
Laurie Paige

#734 BETTER TO HAVE LOVED
Linda Varner

#735 VENUS DE MOLLY
Peggy Webb

 *Silhouette Romance*®

Diana Palmer's fortieth story for Silhouette...chosen
as an Award of Excellence title!

CONNAL
Diana Palmer

Next month, Diana Palmer's bestselling LONG, TALL
TEXANS series continues with CONNAL. The skies
get cloudy on C. C. Tremayne's home on the range
when Penelope Mathews decides to protect him—by
marrying him!

One specially selected title receives the Award of
Excellence every month. Look for CONNAL in August
at your favorite retail outlet...only from Silhouette
Romance.

CON-1

SILHOUETTE'S "BIG WIN"
SWEEPSTAKES RULES & REGULATIONS
NO PURCHASE NECESSARY TO ENTER OR RECEIVE A PRIZE

1. To enter and join the Reader Service, scratch off the metallic strips on all your BIG WIN tickets #1–#6. This will reveal the values for each sweepstakes entry number, the number of free book(s) you will receive, and your free bonus gift as part of our Reader Service. If you do not wish to take advantage of our Reader Service, but wish to enter the Sweepstakes only, scratch off the metallic strips on your BIG WIN tickets #1–#4. Return your entire sheet of tickets intact. Incomplete and/or inaccurate entries are ineligible for that section or sections of prizes. Not responsible for mutilated or unreadable entries or inadvertent printing errors. Mechanically reproduced entries are null and void.

2. Whether you take advantage of this offer or not, your Sweepstakes numbers will be compared against a list of winning numbers generated at random by the computer. In the event that all prizes are not claimed by March 31, 1992, a random drawing will be held from all qualified entries received from March 30, 1990 to March 31, 1992, to award all unclaimed prizes. All cash prizes (Grand to Sixth) will be mailed to the winners and are payable by cheque in U.S. funds. Seventh prize to be shipped to winners via third-class mail. These prizes are in addition to any free, surprise or mystery gifts that might be offered. Versions of this sweepstakes with different prizes of approximate equal value may appear in other mailings or at retail outlets by Torstar Corp. and its affiliates.

3. The following prizes are awarded in this sweepstakes: ★ Grand Prize (1) $1,000,000; First Prize (1) $35,000; Second Prize (1) $10,000; Third Prize (5) $5,000; Fourth Prize (10) $1,000; Fifth Prize (100) $250; Sixth Prize (2500) $10; ★ ★ Seventh Prize (6000) $12.95 ARV.

   ★ This Sweepstakes contains a Grand Prize offering of $1,000,000 annuity. Winner will receive $33,333.33 a year for 30 years without interest totalling $1,000,000.

   ★ ★ Seventh Prize: A fully illustrated hardcover book published by Torstar Corp. Approximate value of the book is $12.95.

   Entrants may cancel the Reader Service at any time without cost or obligation to buy (see details in center insert card).

4. This promotion is being conducted under the supervision of Marden-Kane, Inc., an independent judging organization. By entering this Sweepstakes, each entrant accepts and agrees to be bound by these rules and the decisions of the judges, which shall be final and binding. Odds of winning in the random drawing are dependent upon the total number of entries received. Taxes, if any, are the sole responsibility of the winners. Prizes are nontransferable. All entries must be received by no later than 12:00 NOON, on March 31, 1992. The drawing for all unclaimed sweepstakes prizes will take place May 30, 1992, at 12:00 NOON, at the offices of Marden-Kane, Inc., Lake Success, New York.

5. This offer is open to residents of the U.S., the United Kingdom, France and Canada, 18 years or older except employees and their immediate family members of Torstar Corp., its affiliates, subsidiaries, Marden-Kane, Inc., and all other agencies and persons connected with conducting this Sweepstakes. All Federal, State and local laws apply. Void wherever prohibited or restricted by law. Any litigation respecting the conduct and awarding of a prize in this publicity contest may be submitted to the Régie des loteries et courses du Québec.

6. Winners will be notified by mail and may be required to execute an affidavit of eligibility and release which must be returned within 14 days after notification or, an alternative winner will be selected. Canadian winners will be required to correctly answer an arithmetical skill-testing question administered by mail which must be returned within a limited time. Winners consent to the use of their names, photographs and/or likenesses for advertising and publicity in conjunction with this and similar promotions without additional compensation.

7. For a list of major winners, send a stamped, self-addressed envelope to: WINNERS LIST, c/o MARDEN-KANE, INC., P.O. BOX 701, SAYREVILLE, NJ 08871. Winners Lists will be fulfilled after the May 30, 1992 drawing date.

If Sweepstakes entry form is missing, please print your name and address on a 3″×5″ piece of plain paper and send to:

In the U.S.
Silhouette's "BIG WIN" Sweepstakes
901 Fuhrmann Blvd.
P.O. Box 1867
Buffalo, NY 14269-1867

In Canada
Silhouette's "BIG WIN" Sweepstakes
P.O. Box 609
Fort Erie, Ontario
L2A 5X3

Offer limited to one per household.
© 1989 Harlequin Enterprises Limited   Printed in the U.S.A.

LTY-S790RR

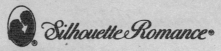

Silhouette Romance®

A duo by Laurie Paige

There's no place like home—and Laurie Paige's delightful duo captures the heartwarming feeling in two special stories set in Arizona ranchland. Share the poignant homecomings of two lovely heroines—half sisters Lainie and Tess—as they travel on the road to romance with their rugged, handsome heroes.

A SEASON FOR HOMECOMING—Lainie and Dev's story...available in June

HOME FIRES BURNING BRIGHT—Tess and Carson's story...available now

Come home to A SEASON FOR HOMECOMING (#727) and HOME FIRES BURNING BRIGHT (#733) . . . only from Silhouette Romance!

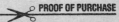